Samantha Alexander lives in Lincolnshire with a variety of animals, including her thoroughbred horse, Bunny, and her two kittens, Cedric and Bramble. Her schedule is almost as busy and exciting as her plots – she writes a number of columns for newspapers and magazines, is a teenage agony aunt for BBC Radio Leeds and in her spare time she regularly competes in dressage and showjumping.

# RIDING SCHOOL

## 1
# Jodie

### SAMANTHA ALEXANDER

MACMILLAN CHILDREN'S BOOKS

First published 1999 by Macmillan Children's Books
a division of Macmillan Publishers Limited
25 Eccleston Place, London SW1W 9NF
Basingstoke and Oxford
www.macmillan.co.uk

Associated companies throughout the world

ISBN 0 330 36836 2

5 7 9 8 6 4

A CIP catalogue record for this book is available from
the British Library.

Phototypeset by Intype London Limited
Printed and bound in Great Britain by
Mackays of Chatham plc, Chatham, Kent

*Samantha Alexander and Macmillan Children's Books would like to thank all at Suzanne's Riding School, especially Suzanne Marczak.*

# Chapter One

"Mum, stop fussing!" I snapped as my stomach somersaulted with a fresh wave of nerves. "Honestly, I'm not an invalid."

The car jerked to a halt outside the high wrought-iron gates and I immediately unfastened the seat belt. An oblong wooden sign swung in the breeze: BROOK HOUSE RIDING SCHOOL. The B in Brook had cracked and all but peeled off.

We'd arrived. There was no turning back now.

"For heaven's sake, Jodie, you're lucky to be alive." My mother touched my arm as if to hold me back. "Aren't I at least entitled to worry?"

"I'll be all right." I fixed a grin on my face and reached for my lunch box and grooming bag on the back seat, avoiding her eyes. "Trust me, I'll ring if anything goes wrong. But it won't. I'm fine."

Her face showed her concern, but she let her hand fall and shooed me out of the car, trying to hide the raw panic which consumed her at the mere mention of horses.

"Mum, I've got to do this." I squeezed her hand

1

and tried to smile reassuringly. "By myself, I've got to prove . . ."

"I know, I know, go on, get out of here." She waved her hand dismissively, staring straight ahead. I stepped out of the car and slung the grooming bag over my shoulder.

"Jodie?"

"Yeah?" I hovered by the half-open door, feeling like it was the first day at a new school.

"Just be careful, that's all your dad and I ask."


"It's crazy! Half the eleven o'clock ride have cancelled, there are no rides tomorrow afternoon . . . At this rate we'll be shut by the end of the week, never mind the end of the year."

"Sssh," another voice chipped in, "there's someone there."

I knocked on the office door and felt a flush of embarrassment creep up my neck. It was so obvious I'd been listening. The door swung open to reveal two girls, one sitting behind a desk, about my age, with thick black hair, the other tall and pretty, perched on a filing cabinet, swinging her legs which were dazzling in bright yellow jean jods.

"Um . . ." I hesitated. "I'm looking for the owner. I was told to come . . ."

"She's not here!" the dark-haired girl fired back. There was no mistaking the irritated tone in her voice. "What do you want?"

"Um, I . . ." I could feel my hands starting to sweat. "I'm the new girl. I was told to be here by nine."

"Oh great, that's all we need." The dark-haired girl slammed the diary shut with unnecessary force. "Look, I don't know what Mrs Brentford's told you but we don't need any more helpers." Disappointment crashed around inside me. I'd been waiting for this day for two and a half years.

The pretty blond girl shifted uneasily, shooting critical looks at her friend. "Why don't you hang around for a few hours?" she suggested hesitantly. "Now that you're here, I'm sure we can find something for you to do." I just wanted the floor to open up and swallow me. The tension in the room was unbearable. "I'll show you round." She jumped off the filing cabinet, pulling on a pair of riding boots.

"Well, if you're going to hang around," the other girl sniped, "there are twenty-four hay nets that need filling. I'm sure Sophie will show you where they are."

"Take no notice of Kate." The other girl took my arm and guided me towards the first row of stables. I instantly liked her warmth and her easy way of talking as if she'd known you for ever.

"Kate's really bossy and it upsets most people. She's got an uncle in Hong Kong who owns race-horses and he's buying her an Arab for her fifteenth

3

birthday. I think it's gone to her head. But she's all right mostly."

We stopped at the first stable which said Rocket above the door. Most riding schools display the names of their horses so people coming for rides can find their mount. A 14.2 chestnut with a squiggly stripe down his nose stuck out his head and nuzzled Sophie's pockets.

"Rocket's really fast and a good jumper," Sophie explained. "Everybody wants to ride him." My hand trembled as I reached out and touched a horse for the first time since the accident. He rubbed the top of his head against my hand and it felt soft and familiar. The smell of hay and leather and horse enveloped me and my eyes filled with tears as emotion threatened to take over.

"Are you all right?" Sophie suddenly looked really concerned. "Only you look as if you've seen a ghost."

"Oats are a traditional feed that can make ponies very excitable. True or false?" A plumpish girl in multicoloured leggings and an "I Love Milton" T-shirt darted out the question as soon as we walked into the saloon.

"False." Sophie rolled her eyes at me after deliberately giving the wrong answer. "Emma talks non-stop and has the attention span of a five-year-old." Sophie bounded forward and pulled the copy

4

of *In the Saddle* out of her hand. "She also has an obsession with a pony called Buzby who would have a criminal record and an IQ of zero if he were human."

"Don't be a pig." Emma grabbed for the magazine, hurt flickering over her face.

"Oh Emm!" Sophie read the quiz. "You haven't even got one of these questions right!"

Sophie and I had just spent an hour trudging around with a leading rein class, walking stubborn ponies through heavy sand. The instructor, who worked part-time, kept losing her temper and didn't seem the slightest bit bothered when one of the smallest riders got caught on a bramble and was nearly pulled out of the saddle.

Sophie had giggled and desperately tried to lead a piebald called Foxy. I was leading a gorgeous little Connemara called Blossom who quickly learned she could lean on my arm. The boy who was riding her kept kicking me in the back when I didn't run fast enough so I was quite pleased when Blossom eventually tipped him off.

"If I have to prepare to trot and trot on one more time," I groaned, "I shall go mad."

Sophie shot me a quizzical look and then pulled me over to a corner by the window on the pretext of looking at riding hats. "Listen," she said, "I couldn't help noticing your leg."

"What?" I yelped, immediately on the defensive.

"If you've hurt yourself, you shouldn't be running up and down like that. Don't let Kate bully you."

"I'm not. I mean, it's just a sprain." All the old feelings of humiliation rose up and I had to take a deep breath to get a grip. "I'm fine," I lied. "As I said, it's just a sprain."

"Are you a horse-brain or just a beginner?" Emma plonked herself down next to me and bit into a banana and peanut butter sandwich.

"Um, neither really." I felt my spirits hurtling to the ground. My first day back at riding school wasn't meant to be like this.

The saloon was a converted stable with western-style louvred doors and a long table in the middle. There were posters of horses everywhere and piles of bags and riding gear in the corner. It smelt of dust and desperately needed a good clean.

"So do you own a pony or what?"

Emma didn't stop talking for one second, mainly about Buzby who she obviously worshipped, and about the other girls in the yard. Every muscle in my body ached. I was completely out of shape and had never worked so hard in my life. Kate had pushed me from the start, rattling out orders to do all the jobs that everyone hated. Scrubbing mangers, sweeping the yard, levelling the muck heap, cleaning horse rugs. I'd put up with about all I could take. Brook House had to be the worst run riding school in the whole country. It was a nightmare.

"Take no notice of Kate." Emma dropped her voice and leaned close, seeming to tune into my thoughts. "She gives every new girl a hard time – it's like her own personal initiation ceremony." Emma wrinkled her freckled nose and glanced around as if to check Kate wasn't there.

"Oh," I murmured, relief flooding through me. "I thought I was the only one she didn't like."

"Jodie, Jodie, where are you?" Kate's deep authoritative voice bellowed out from behind the door.

"Speak of the devil," I groaned, wanting to dive under the table for cover. "Doesn't she ever give anyone a break?"

Kate marched in through the louvred doors just as Emma dropped half her sandwich on the floor.

"Oh, you're in here. I might have known." Kate eyed the mess with a look of disdain. She had a way of tucking her dark hair behind her ears and sticking out her chin which made her seem ultra-important. "Frank needs tacking up," she ordered. "And while you're at it, you can give him a good brush." There was still no sign of Mrs Brentford or of Sandra the (full-time) groom, and the riding instructor had disappeared on the pretext of picking up her cat from the vet.

Frank was a part-Shire, gentle giant with feet like

7

breeze-blocks and a really gormless expression. He looked after the novice adult riders who were either terribly nervous or fancied themselves as a Frankie Dettori. Even if a bomb went off, Frank would still have a one-paced plod. According to Sophie nobody liked tacking him up because the saddle was so heavy and you had to stand on a bucket to reach his back.

"Yes sir." I saluted Kate's departing figure. One more order and I was going to tell her where to go.

The tack room was up a flight of stone steps above the stables. There were neat rows of saddle racks and bridle hooks with a horse's name next to each, and various bandages, boots and martingales thrown all over the place. Frank's bridle was in pieces on top of his saddle and I only needed one guess as to who had undone it.

I picked up the headpiece and browband and methodically fitted it back together, remembering to keep the bit the right way and the noseband on the inside of the cheekpieces. It would take more than a dismantled bridle to catch me out.

Voices in the stable below drifted up just as I looped the reins through the throat lash.

"Do you think she knows what she's doing?"

It was Sophie. Without a doubt. I stayed absolutely still and recognized Emma's voice mentioning Buzby. They can't have realized I was still in the tack room.

"Don't tell anyone," Sophie said in a hushed whisper, "but when I showed her Rocket she nearly freaked. I thought she was going to burst into tears. And when I suggested we rode bareback to the field she was petrified. I don't think she can ride."

White-hot anger mixed with bitter resentment boiled to the surface. How dare they talk about me behind my back? I thought they were decent – I thought they were possible future friends.

Grabbing Frank's saddle and bridle, blinded by tears, I stumbled for the door. I didn't notice that the reins were dangling down.

"Watch out!" Kate looked up from the yard just as I lost my footing. My knees buckled and I tipped forward but I couldn't right myself. The steps swirled into a blur as a sudden needling cramp shot up my left leg.

There was nothing I could do. My whole leg had seized up.

The saddle crashed downwards pommel first, stirrups flying, as I released an arm to grab for the handrail. The noise was horrendous. It crashed down each step, scuffing on the rough stone, bruising from the sheer force. It could have been me.

Kate moved forwards in slow motion, her wide, horrified eyes never leaving the saddle. After what seemed like minutes it bounced off the last couple of steps. I heard a sickening crack as the wooden tree under the leather snapped in half and it rolled limp onto the concrete.

"What have you done?" Kate ran forward and then shrank back from the misshapen heap as if it were a dead bird. Sophie and Emma dashed out of the stable, open-mouthed with shock. At least they'd noticed that I was doubled up, clutching my left leg and trying to drag myself down the steps on my bottom one at a time.

"It's ruined . . . You idiot!" A wave of anger darkened Kate's features.

But it was too late. I'd had more than I could take.

"Don't say a word," I hissed, halting halfway down the steps and gritting my teeth to keep a brave face. "You can stick your stupid riding school, and all your lousy jobs. Even convicts wouldn't want to work here. It's the unfriendliest place on earth." I was really buzzing now, letting it all rush out. "I thought horsy people helped each other. Well all you lot do is snipe and pick holes in people. You're pathetic, all of you, and it's no wonder nobody rides here. It's a shambles. It's the stables from hell, it's . . ."

"Have you quite finished?" Kate glared at me, her eyes wide.

"No, I haven't," I yelled. "Not until I collect my stuff and get out of here. And good riddance."

I made a superhuman effort to drag myself up

and then limped across to the saloon feeling their eyes boring into my back.

Inside, I slammed the door and then leaned back, my breath coming in short gasps. I closed my eyes and slowly slid down the door, wrapping my arms round my legs and burying my head in my knees. Hot tears trickled down my cheeks, followed by rasping sobs and long shudders of emptiness.

I'd waited for this day for so long. After the accident the surgeon had told my mother that nothing could be done and most of the nerves in my leg had been damaged. Two six-hour operations followed. I'd smashed my lower leg in seven different places. The surgeon was nothing less than brilliant. I couldn't move my toes for over a year but I had a superb physiotherapist who I worked desperately hard for. Over my bed was a picture of a chestnut Arab and it was the driving ambition to ride again which kept me going.

Brook House Riding School was meant to fulfil that dream. It had never occurred to me that it might not be like my old stables. I'd thought that I could slip back into my past life. But that wasn't meant to be.

The only thing I was sure about at that moment was that I'd never come back to this riding school. Not in a thousand years and not if they paid me a million pounds. Not ever.

# Chapter Two

"There are two girls to see you." Mum pushed open my bedroom door completely ignoring the *Do not disturb* sign. "You never told me you'd made some friends." She practically pushed me off the bed and started puffing up the pillows.

"I haven't," I snapped, trying not to show my red swollen eyes. "And I'm not here. Tell them they've got the wrong house."

I'd already spotted Emma and Sophie hovering in the driveway. They were still in their riding gear so they'd obviously come straight from the stables. Of course, my address and phone number were in the appointment book.

"I'm not going to start lying for you, Jodie." Mum straightened up, giving the room one final appraisal. "I don't approve of you riding again, you know that, and I don't know what's gone on today at the stables, but how many times have I told you, you can't run away from your problems."

"Millions." I stared out of the window, scowling. "Well then, I'll send them up."

"Can we come in?" Sophie knocked nervously on my half-open door and peered round the gap. She was uneasy with embarrassment and Emma clung on behind like a scared rabbit. Despite myself I softened, just a little.

"Wow!" Emma caught a glimpse of my model horse collection and all her inhibitions flew out of the window. "These are so cool." She was at my dressing table in seconds admiring Black Beauty which stood a whole thirty centimetres high. I had fifty-two model and china horses and a miniature stable and paddock with jumps, which was balanced on my bedside table.

"Don't touch." Sophie followed Emma in, padding across the carpet in her socks. While they had their backs turned I hastily shoved a photograph of me riding into my chest of drawers.

"Nice bedroom." Sophie gazed at the horsy posters which were all of famous showjumpers. Underneath, I'd marked in the date, place and rider's name as well as the horse. She squinted slightly and I guessed what she was thinking. I didn't have the usual twelve-year-old's bedroom. Everything was impeccably tidy. Like my dad, I'd always needed everything to be orderly, and after the

13

accident it had become essential to have everything in its place just so I could function.

"Um, we're really sorry about earlier." Sophie fidgeted, twisting her ring round on her middle finger. "Nobody meant to upset you."

"If it's about the saddle I'll pay for the repairs." I tried to make my voice as cold as possible. I didn't let on that I hadn't got a penny to my name. I'd just have to get a job.

"No, no, it's not that," Sophie stammered, casting her eyes down. "Kate didn't mean to be so nasty, it's just that she's trying her best for the stables."

"What, by getting rid of customers?" I deliberately loaded my voice with sarcasm.

"No, it's—"

"Coffee!" Mum burst in with a tray of mugs and biscuits and I nearly died of embarrassment. "We've only been here three weeks." She started on our life story before she'd even put the tray down. "Most of the furniture is still in storage. I expect Jodie will be going to the same school as you in September."

"Mum," I hissed, breaking out in a sweat, "we're having a serious conversation here."

"Oh, righty-ho. Well, I'll just go and polish the bathroom tiles then." She winked at me as she went out and I caught Sophie smiling.

Dad was an engineer working in India for two months at a time and we'd moved to Limestone

14

Avenue so Mum could be nearer her family. My brother loved it because there was a bowling alley just down the road and a football pitch. I hated it because it didn't have a paddock and I'd left all my friends behind.

"Brook House is in trouble," Emma blurted out as soon as the door was closed. Sophie glared at her but she carried on. "Look, we might as well tell her," Emma insisted. "It's hardly a well-kept secret."

"Horseworld Centre opened about a year ago," Sophie said, taking over the story, "and it's taken all the business. They've got an indoor school and young flashy ponies and, well, Brook House can't compete. It looks unlikely that Mrs Brentwood will be able to feed the horses this winter. She's absolutely broke."

I remembered Horseworld Centre. There were big adverts in the evening paper but when I rang up to enquire, the lessons were expensive and they didn't let anyone help out.

"So why are you telling me?" I was trying hard not to look interested.

"Because we care about the horses." Emma was getting really passionate. "Because half of them are too old to start a new life and the other half are either too badly behaved or set in their ways. Rusty is ancient, Ebony Jane's taught so many people to ride she deserves a medal. Tinky wouldn't

15

last two minutes in a new home, Monty is a crib-
biter and Elvis and Faldo aren't even broken in
yet." She was flushed and tears shone in her eyes.
"They all love each other though. They're a family
and they don't deserve to be split up. They'd end up
at some horse market being sold for meat and we
can't let that happen." She shuddered at the thought
of it and Sophie reached out and touched her
shoulder.

And I knew I'd been touched too – in my heart.

"Mrs Brentford's given up hope," Sophie explained. "She doesn't know what to do for the best."

"If the school closes down it will break her
heart," Emma added, her mouth quivering.

"But I don't see," I said, slumping on the bed.
"What can *I* do? Why are you telling *me* this?"

"Because we want you to join our gang." Sophie
stared straight at me. "There are five of us – Rachel
and Steph you haven't met. We're all determined to
save the riding school."

"We were really impressed by all your hard
work," Emma explained. "We call ourselves the
Five Pack, and we'd like you to join us."

"And Kate's in agreement?" I asked doubtfully.

"Well, not exactly," Sophie hedged.

"She's been outvoted," Emma jumped in. "You
don't have to ride, just throw in some ideas."

"It took us an extra bus ride and half Emma's
pocket money to find you," Sophie pleaded.

16

I decided not to mention overhearing their conversation in the tack room.

"So, are you in or what?" Emma demanded.

"Have you any kind of a plan?" I asked.

"Nothing." Sophie shrugged. "We haven't got a clue what to do."

I reached out my hand. Emma put hers on top and Sophie placed hers on top of Emma's.

"The Six Pack," I said.

"The Six Pack."

"And I'll try not to freak out when I see the horses," I said, grinning.

Needless to say, they both cringed with embarrassment.

"This is Rachel, and that's Steph."

Sophie shuffled awkwardly as Steph barely acknowledged me and carried on tacking up a pretty grey pony called Monty.

"She can be a bit awkward sometimes," Sophie apologized, breathing a sigh of relief when Steph mounted and rode off to the manege. "I think she's got family problems. Monty's on part-loan at the riding stables but her dad wants to get rid of him."

"That must be awful." I really felt for her.

"Yeah, but Steph's not the kind of girl you can feel sorry for. She shuts everybody out, and to be quite honest, she thinks she's it."

All five girls were having an hour's group lesson with the instructor, Janice, in return for helping Sandra out over the weekend. I was dying to get up in the saddle but didn't dare try in front of everybody. Yesterday I'd taxed the wasted muscles in my calf and now I was suffering the consequences.

Rachel led out Rusty who was an ancient roan pony but with the sweetest face I'd ever seen. His thick tail fanned out behind and his eyes were hidden behind a thatch of black mane. Rachel tied it up in a bobble so "he could see where he was going".

Rachel was small with long brown hair. She was eleven and crippled by shyness. She wasn't unfriendly but when I tried to make conversation she blushed deeply and shot under Rusty's saddle flap to tighten the girth.

Sophie was explaining how to stretch one of Rusty's forelegs forward so as to even out any wrinkled skin caught under the girth. Sophie spoke gently and Rachel listened quietly, taking it all in. She obviously hadn't been riding for very long.

Rusty was the perfect beginner's pony and stood half dozing, as solid as a rock.

"Rachel lives near you," Sophie said, turning towards me. "Perhaps you could give each other lifts, organize some kind of a rota."

The colour drained from Rachel's face and a flicker of real fear filled her eyes. "Or perhaps not,"

I hastily added. Sophie and I shared a look, wondering what on earth had caused such a reaction.

"Don't start without me!" Emma charged up the drive clutching a pink and black crop and wearing an oversized T-shirt with a photograph of Buzby printed on the front. The back read *Pony in a Million* and *Stable Star of the Year*. I looked up and saw the real Buzby's head appear over a stable door with his bridle slipped over one ear where he'd obviously been rubbing. He gave Emma a delighted squeal and started kicking wildly at the door. I tried to cover up an angry purple bruise on my arm where he had sunk his teeth in just minutes earlier, all because I didn't have a titbit for him.

"I overslept." Emma ran straight towards him, her cheeks pink with excitement. "I couldn't sleep, I've got so many ideas. Oh, Buz—" She stopped suddenly and her face fell. "I've forgotten your liquorice allsorts!"

The lesson got off to a shaky start, mainly because Buzby, in a really bad mood, kept bulldozing into Monty's behind. As a result Monty bucked Steph off.

"Keep your distance!" Janice screeched. Steph was nearly in tears because she thought she'd broken a tooth. Emma was trotting round and round with her reins like washing lines, completely out of control.

"OK, that's it, everyone turn in." Janice sounded murderous. "How many times do I have to tell you to keep a horse a good distance from the ride ahead. You should be able to see the hocks of the pony in front."

Steph glared at Emma who was quivering like a jelly because Buzby had decided it was the ideal moment for a good shake.

"Has anybody got any questions?" Janice asked. Emma stuck up her hand but the instructor had already turned her back. "Prepare to walk and walk on."

They all set off around the school with Kate leading file on Archie who was a palomino with a really cheeky expression. According to Emma, he and Buzby were inseparable and sure enough, Buzby wouldn't settle until he was following Archie nose to tail.

Kate was definitely the better rider but then she was the oldest at thirteen. She concentrated hard and had a nice seat and rhythm. Archie could be really good if he'd stop acting the fool and pay attention.

Sophie had a natural advantage with really long legs which wrapped around the pony's sides, but she tended to lean too far back and have her reins too long.

"OK, circle to the rear of the ride in turn." Janice made no secret of the fact she was bored rigid.

When it came to Rachel's turn, Rusty was a bit slow and had to trot to catch up with the rest of the ride. Janice singled her out and made her do it again which caused Rachel to turn bright red and lose her stirrups.

"Give him a kick, Rachel, for goodness' sake." Janice nagged constantly which only made her go to pieces and ride worse than ever.

"Rachel always holds us back," Steph muttered to Sophie as she rode past giving Monty a boot in the ribs with her outside leg.

But Rachel finally got the gist of what Janice was saying and got Rusty moving forward. Only I noticed that she was close to tears and utterly mortified.

Emma didn't stop talking for the whole lesson which made me want to gag her. I'd already decided that Janice was a terrible instructor lacking any kind of discipline, enthusiasm or encouragement. By the time they got on to jumping, it was complete chaos with everyone shooting off in different directions. I decided to sneak off before Janice collared me into helping with the poles and found something else to criticize.

We were having a meeting in the saloon straight after the lesson but that still gave me fifteen minutes to have a good look around the school. Up until now I'd only seen the yard and the manege. I wanted

21

to familiarize myself with all the different horses and ponies and with the facilities. At that moment I had no idea of the shock that was in store for me. I had no idea that my life was about to change for ever.

There were eight horses and thirteen ponies at Brook House, all varying in size from a Shetland to a Shire, and all different types, which was a good thing. It was quite obvious though that the ones who'd been schooled had clearly forgotten it, and the others had just blasted through life, eating, sleeping and behaving badly.

The two New Forest ponies, Elvis and Faldo, were in a four acre field with the rest of the ponies and were having a tussle with a little Shetland who was quite clearly the boss. They were dark brown with tiny white stars on their foreheads and long unpulled manes which I was itching to get my hands into. They had no idea about basic good manners and grabbed at my arm, eager for horse nuts.

I took out my notebook and jotted down various details, then moved on to the horse paddock where big Frank was dozing under a horse chestnut tree. Ebony Jane, the ex-racehorse, was standing next to him and the other horses were clustered around the water trough.

Sophie had already told me that it was the children rather than the adults who had defected to Horseworld Centre. In the week they still had quite a good turnover of office workers and housewives, keen to take up a glamorous hobby, but at weekends and in the holidays, the ponies were standing idle, and that's where Brook House had made most of its money before.

There was a corrugated barn at the back of a row of stables half full of hay and straw. A couple of fields had been cut for hay but it obviously wasn't enough to last the winter. I noted down that some cross-country fences had become overgrown and it would be a good idea to clear the weeds and get them back in use.

I was just thinking about going back to the saloon and waiting for the girls when a flicker of movement on the other side of a thick thorn hedge caught my eye. I knew it was a horse but I couldn't work out why it was separated from the others. A bright red chestnut body flickered through the foliage and I heard a loud impatient snort. My heart skipped a beat and I dropped my notebook.

If I could just push through a gap I'd be into the field. The horse started trotting towards me. I dropped down onto my hands and knees and shuffled and scraped under the barbed wire. I had to push blind through some creeper which was blocking the view. My shoulders squeezed through a foot-wide gap in the hedge. I could hear the horse pawing and snorting, obviously hearing me too. I

23

grabbed at a handful of sticky creeper and that was it – I was through.

"Whoa boy, whoa, steady there." My heart beat wildly with excitement. I was staring at the most beautiful chestnut Arab I'd ever seen.

He was exactly the same as the picture above my bed. His lovely dished face tapered down to soft black flared nostrils showing pink inside. Every nerve in his body was tensed ready to spring away. I could barely breathe with emotion. He was incredible. He was a vision.

I scrabbled onto my feet far too fast and he shied away, the long, fiery-red tail splaying out over his back. Despite his fear he was overcome with curiosity, and after a few minutes took a tentative step forward to sniff at my outstretched hand. His breath was hot and wary, but unable to resist, he snatched at the horse nuts in my hand and then backed off.

"Whoa boy, whoa now, I'm not going to hurt you." I had a job keeping my voice steady as I was trembling all over. He pawed the ground and I offered him another handful, his whiskers tickling my palm as his lips fumbled velvet soft and he took the food. I knew he was checking me out as much as anything else but he stayed put and that had to count for something.

My brain reeled with possible explanations. A riding school would never have an Arab like this as one of the school horses. He'd be far too lively. I didn't even know if this was Mrs Brentford's field. He could belong to somebody else, anyone in the surrounding area.

At a rough guess I'd say he was about 14.2 hands. Tenderly I reached out and ran my hand down the impressive long silky mane which trailed the top of his shoulder. Then, with a jolt I realized – that thick crested neck, the sheer power and energy – he wasn't just an ordinary horse, he was a stallion!

"Jodie!" Kate's voice sliced through my whirring thoughts. It brought me crashing down to earth. The meeting! They must have finished ages ago. "Jodie, is that you?"

I scrabbled back through the hedge, snagging my sweatshirt on the wire. "Just one second," I croaked, getting entwined in creeper.

Kate was waiting on the other side, her arms crossed in front of her, feigning boredom, her hair still flattened and sweaty from the riding hat.

"You've got to tell me," I blurted out, brushing down my jeans, still in a state of excitement. "Who does that horse belong to?"

Kate's face registered surprise. "You mean she hasn't told you?"

"Who? What?" I didn't follow her.

"Well, well." The smugness flooding into Kate's face was unmistakeable. I could see her choosing her words carefully for maximum impact. "The

25

horse is called Minstrel." She hesitated, drawing breath, scrutinizing my face for every movement. "And as you are obviously completely unaware," she continued, a triumphant smile playing on her lips, "he belongs to Sophie."

# Chapter Three

"Treasure hunt, picnics, Own a Pony Week, Western riding, barbecue, quiz nights . . ." Emma reeled off the ideas from her list, gesticulating wildly with her free hand to emphasize each point. Kate and I barged in through the louvred doors, red-faced and out of breath.

"Why not just bring in the Household Cavalry and be done with it?" Steph pretended to yawn and flicked through *Smash Hits* focusing all her attention on a picture of Peter Andre.

"We've only got the summer holidays," Kate butted in, "and whatever plans we come up with have got to be cleared with Mrs Brentford."

"Oh come on." Steph looked up, all superior. "She's more interested in her bridge parties and playing golf than Brook House. We could paint all the stables pink and she wouldn't notice."

"That's not true." Emma leapt to her defence. "She's just lost all her fight – she doesn't know what to do."

"Oh yeah, let's see if you still say that next time

she gives you a mouthful for leaving baling string all over the place."

Sophie sat in the corner, doodling on an old newspaper. All I could think of was Minstrel. How could she turn her back on such a fabulous horse? I felt sick. Last night I'd been so excited, bursting with ideas and determination. Now I just felt let down and a complete fool. How could she be a friend if she kept something from me that was so important? Yesterday afternoon we'd talked for hours about our favourite horses and not a word about Minstrel.

"There's the annual Brook House Show and Gymkhana." Kate immediately took over. "That's always a success, and it's a good opportunity to recruit new riders—"

"Excuse me," Sophie interrupted, sticking up her hand, "but last year Archie bucked off three novices and Buzby wouldn't move in the gymkhana races. They're hardly a good advertisement for well-behaved ponies, are they?"

"I think the first thing we've got to do is clean up the place." I stood up and spoke for the first time. The silence seemed to go on for ever. Rachel, who hadn't said a word so far, coughed nervously.

"Look, I know you're just trying to help," said Kate in her condescending voice, "but I think it's going to take a lot more than knocking down a few cobwebs to save the school." Steph giggled and

28

Emma and Sophie stared out of the window, refusing to give me any support.

"Well, um, actually, I agree." Rachel's voice wobbled with nerves. Everyone turned round and stared as if it had been the chair that had spoken and not Rachel. Kate glared, her eyebrows shooting up. "Well, nobody likes riding somewhere shabby, do they?" Rachel was starting to blush and squirmed uneasily under the laser rays coming from Kate.

Steph tossed back her bouncy dark blond hair and made a kind of deep guttural snort. The girl was obviously obnoxious but I still wasn't prepared for her cutting, spiteful remark. "Well, we'll buy you two a bottle of bleach and a bucket but if you don't mind we'll concentrate on more important issues like finding new riders."

I winced as if physically stung.

"Hey, that's a bit rough." Sophie finally leapt to my defence, but it was too late.

"Well, you do that." My voice trembled and I tried to fight the urge to run out of the saloon. "Because this five pack, six pack thing you've got going is a load of rubbish. You're not interested in the horses, you just want to score points off each other. And every moment you squabble, every hour you spend fighting means there's less and less chance of the horses having a roof over their heads. You say you care about Buzby, about Archie, Rocket,

29

Rusty, but all you really care about is yourselves, about who's the best. Well, it makes me sick. And when Brook House closes down I hope you'll be really proud of yourselves."

Kate gaped and Steph sat speechless. Emma started smirking and immediately stuck up her hand. "When do we begin?" She beamed, delighted that I'd put Kate in her place.

"The long-term plan is to be voted Riding School of the Year." I was going to pull out my notebook but decided against it.

"We could be in a photo story for *In the Saddle*," Sophie suggested, trying to be supportive, but I couldn't even look her in the eye.

"We could form our own pony club!" said Emma.

"And who says Brook House is closing down?" The deep authoritative voice from the doorway made everyone jump. I turned round to see a tiny sparrow-like woman with grey wispy hair.

"I'd like to see Jodie Williams in the house, right now," she boomed, her beady eyes darting round the room.

"That's Mrs Brentford," Emma mouthed, as soon as she'd turned on her heel and clipped off towards the house.

"Oh great," I groaned, feeling weary with dread. "I thought you said she was nice?"

"You've blown it now." Kate pushed past me,

looking as if she wanted to cheer. "She'll eat you for breakfast."

"Good luck." Rachel smiled warmly, oozing sympathy. Sophie hung back, pretending to rearrange some plastic chairs. Emma linked arms and frog-marched me out of the saloon and towards the house. I felt like Mary, Queen of Scots going off to be beheaded.

"Just stay calm." Emma fluttered around nervously. "You'll be fine. It's quite an honour to be invited into the house, you know." She desperately tried to fish for good points but failed miserably.

"What, even though I'm probably going to be banned from ever coming here again and given a bill for a new saddle?"

"Look on the bright side of life, why don't you?" Emma clutched my hand and dragged me along the side of a privet hedge to a small gate. "Just smile sweetly and agree with everything she says."

"And what if I don't?"

"Then you still smile sweetly and agree with everything she says?"

I braced myself and opened the little gate which was covered in delicate pink roses. The whole framework shuddered and creaked on its hinges and a flurry of petals cascaded to the ground.

"Wish me luck." I half turned back.

"Break a leg." Emma stuck up her thumb and I had to smile at the irony.

31

I walked up the cottage path and knocked on the faded green door, shocked at just how much I wanted to keep coming here. I was hooked whether I liked it or not.

"That was quite a speech you gave in there." Mrs Brentford bustled me into the kitchen down some stone steps, telling me to mind my head as I went. She had to be less then five feet tall but carried herself with a grace and a poise which made her seem much taller. Entering the kitchen was like stepping back in time. There was an old stone sink and an Aga and a big wooden table in the middle with a rocking chair pulled up at one end.

"So Riding School of the Year, eh? That's some task you've set yourself." She put on a pair of glasses hanging round her neck on a string which looked uncannily like an old bootlace, and examined me from top to bottom. "So do you always get so passionate about your beliefs?"

"Only when it concerns horses." I tried to keep my voice level.

"And other people's business by the sound of it."

I squirmed painfully and watched an insect zigzag across the floor. "We didn't know you were there." I murmured so low she almost had to lip-read.

"How old are you?"

"Twelve."

"Sixty-nine." She tapped at her head. "Getting

32

ready for the scrap heap according to my daughter. So what makes you think you can save this riding school when I obviously can't?"

I dragged in my breath, taken aback by her directness. "Well, um, to be honest . . ." I was scrabbling wildly for something to say, but my mind was a total blank.

"I don't bite, at least not after lunch," Mrs Brentford prompted.

"Well, there are six of us and it's the summer holidays. We're enthusiastic and hard-working and we're determined and dedicated. And we owe it to the horses. They've taught so many people to ride, it's not right that they should be split up. They're happy here."

"You could always go to Horseworld Centre." Mrs Brentford sat down heavily in the rocking chair, not taking her eyes off me for a second.

"But all we'd be is a number," I whipped back at her. "We wouldn't be able to groom and hang out and do all the horsy things everybody dreams about. We'd be in and out on a conveyor belt and all we'd have is one measly hour a week. We love horses, Mrs Brentford. All we want is to be around them. Brook House is the only place in the whole area which gives us that chance. And we'll do anything to help. Anything." I broke off, blushing, my breath rattling from nerves. I knew I sounded desperate but I didn't know what else to do. It was how I felt.

33

For a second Mrs Brentford seemed impressed but then she narrowed her eyes, cloaking her real feelings.

"You didn't sound very united in the saloon," she said finally, running the tips of her fingers over her lined forehead. "And then there's the small matter of Frank's saddle . . ."

"I can get a job, I can pay that off," I gulped, digging my fingernails into the sweaty palms of my hands. "I can get a paper round. It wouldn't take many weeks. And as for the girls, we all get on really well, you just caught us at a bad moment." I'd now resorted to telling lies to keep coming to Brook House. "No, that's not exactly true." I took it back. "We don't all get on well, but we still care about the riding school."

A small, thin smile played on Mrs Brentford's lips. "Thank you for being honest, that means a lot." She stood up, scraping back the chair, and brushing down her jumper. "How about I give you one week to clean up the stables, the tack room, feed room and all the ponies. That should pay off the debt, don't you think? You can rope in those other girls and that uppity little Miss Kate and her pal with no manners. I'm sure you can sort them out."

A huge wave of delirious joy rose up inside me. I felt like kissing her on both cheeks.

"And you might as well know," she continued,

waving her hand dismissively, "Janice handed her notice in a few days ago. There won't be any lessons until the end of the week when the new instructor arrives. So, as long as it's OK with Sandra, if you want to ride the ponies every day . . ."

It got better and better.

"The girls will be thrilled." I was on cloud nine.

Mrs Brentford leaned forward, cocking her head slightly and sucking in her cheeks. It was as if she was trying to make a decision.

"Jodie." Her voice softened, her face crinkling like a crumpled-up paper bag. "Your mum rang and told me about the accident."

I felt the euphoria drain out of me as if someone had pulled a plug. "You won't say anything?" I pleaded. "She had no right." I couldn't believe my mother had interfered like that. It was none of her business.

"She was just worried, that's all. It's inevitable."

"But it's my secret, I'm the one who has to live with it. She had no right." I stared blindly towards a corner of the tiled kitchen floor, the old familiar resentment boiling up.

"I'm sorry you feel like that, Jodie, because while you keep it all bottled up inside you like this you'll never get over it and on with your life."

Any confidence I had was engulfed by embarrassment. I stared out of the window struggling like crazy to stop my jaw from shaking.

"You don't know what it's like," I murmured. "In and out of hospital like a yo-yo, this treatment, that treatment, never being able to wear a skirt or shorts, being called a freak at the swimming baths, people staring – you can't even imagine."

I felt hollow inside. A tear slipped down my cheek and into my mouth. It was as if I had a huge wound inside me and Mrs Brentford had just pulled off the scab. "You feel sorry for me." I knew I was being irrational but the words and the hurt came tumbling out. "That's why you're being so nice. I don't want pity. I don't want sympathy. I can't handle it."

"Now you listen to me." Mrs Brentford grabbed my arm. "I don't feel sorry for you, you've had a rough two years but you've still got two legs, two arms, you're healthy and luckier than most. So you've got a metal plate in your leg and the scars to prove it. So what? It's what's in your heart that matters most, in your character." She stepped back, her eyes as hard as bullets. "If anyone's feeling sorry for you, Jodie, it's yourself. You're wallowing in self-pity and if I'm trying to do anything it's make you snap out of it."

I was speechless. Nobody had ever spoken to me like that before, they'd always tiptoed around the subject. I felt raw with outrage but deep down I knew she was close to the truth. "Now I've said all I want to say, the rest is up to you." She turned her back, brushing me off, indicating the conversation was over. Numbly, I fumbled for the door, my shoulders sagging, a thousand thoughts scurrying through my mind.

"Oh and Jodie?"

I jerked upright.

"If you've got anything about you you'll be riding at the Brook House Show in two weeks' time. Don't let a natural talent go to waste."

And not for the first time I wondered just how much my mother had actually told her.

"I can't believe it! Did she really say all that?" Emma was trying to put hoof oil on Buzby but he kept lifting up each foot as soon as she got anywhere near.

"Just think, one whole week of riding." She gave up and sat on the outside tap which Steph said would break under her weight. "We've got to cherish every moment. This is going to be the best week of my entire life."

"Well, I can ride Monty whenever I want," Steph boasted and nearly got a hoof-oil brush in her face.

"I think we ought to start with the tack room," I suggested, already plotting and planning. "It's a pigsty in there."

"Yeah, I agree." Steph wrinkled up her nose. "Emma's been leaving banana skins behind the rug baskets."

"I have not!"

37

"I wonder what the new instructor's going to be like?" said Steph dreamily, no doubt conjuring up pictures of Carl Hester.

"Strict, mean, frumpy, and resembling the back end of a bus," Kate threw in, leading Archie onto a patch of grass. "And has anybody seen my new green lead rope?"

"I also think," I struggled on, "that as the Brook House Show is definitely going ahead, we ought to school the ponies this week for their best events. At least then, they'll stand a chance against the other ponies."

Kate's face blackened and she deliberately ignored me. Steph muttered something under her breath. Even Archie glared at me, a daisy hanging from his mouth. Emma rabbited on about a "pamper day" for Buzby and a mint-flavoured equine football which she was saving up for. Any positive thoughts I was still clinging on to quickly evaporated.

"Has anyone, by any chance," I asked, shooting Kate a withering glance, "heard of the words Troop Motivation?"


"Why didn't you tell me?"

Sophie was in Rocket's stable, keeping a low profile. All the horses were being turned out in the fields for the week but Rocket suffered from sweet itch so he stayed in to avoid the midges. Sweet itch is an allergy to midge bites which causes horses to rub their manes and tails, often until they are raw. Sophie was putting some soothing benzyl benzoate lotion on Rocket but there was more on the door frame and her T-shirt than on his neck.

"You own the next best thing to Milton and you didn't tell me." I still felt hurt and shut out and it came across in my voice.

"Oh." Sophie stiffened visibly, concentrating on picking out bits of straw from an old dandy brush. Her blond hair fell forwards so I couldn't read the expression on her face. It was ages before she spoke. When she did her voice was stilted and shaky. "Let me guess." She finally looked up, meeting my eyes with a mixture of guilt and sadness. "Kate couldn't wait to tell you."

# Chapter Four

"He was a birthday present. I've had him for three months." Sophie sat on the village green bench staring vaguely at a bag of chips.

We'd sneaked off into the village while the other girls weren't looking. There was a Post Office, a fish and chip shop, a mini-supermarket, a newsagent's and a pub. I'd bought a copy of *In the Saddle* which had a picture of the famous event riders Ash Burgess and Alex Johnson on the front cover. According to Emma they lived close by, at a really smart event yard.

Awkwardly, Sophie told me how she'd asked the girls to keep Minstrel a secret because she couldn't stand the million and one questions when people found out.

"I haven't been near Minstrel since the day I got him and that's the way I want it to stay." Her lips tightened and she clenched her hands together. "It's a personal thing between me and my dad, OK?"

I couldn't believe that such a fantastic horse had been turned out in a field for the whole summer. No wonder he was so wild, he was never handled.

Sophie explained how when Minstrel first arrived, everyone thought they could ride him. "Steph was the worst, she put me down all the time, but when I thrust the saddle at her she was terrified. Janice and Sandra both managed to get on him but were bucked off almost immediately."

I listened in grim fascination. "But what on earth made your dad buy you an Arab and a stallion of all things? It's like buying a Ferrari for someone who's just passed their test."

"Because he's stupid and thinks he knows everything, and whoever sold Minstrel to my dad must have seen him coming a hundred miles off." Sophie's voice was full of bitterness.

I leaned back, trying to absorb all the facts, completely blown away by it all. To be overfaced by the wrong horse was the worst thing in the world but I couldn't help feeling sorry for Minstrel. He was a victim too. And he must be so bored and lonely.

A mother and two children walked past to feed the ducks, the kids staring at our jodhpurs and boots with envy. Sophie's hand was gripping on to the armrest of the bench so hard that the knuckles had turned white. "If I still haven't ridden him after six months, Dad said he'd sell him, that's the deal."

"And you've got no intentions of trying?" I asked tentatively.

"The day a horsebox comes to fetch Minstrel will

41

be the best day of my life. I've just got three months to go."

"You hate Minstrel that much?" I said, incredulous.

"I don't hate *him* at all." Sophie pushed her hair behind her ears. "But I hate everything he stands for." She sat staring ahead, biting down on her bottom lip, her eyes screwed up against the sun.

"You know, I mean, I don't want to pry, but sometimes it helps to talk about things."

Sophie forced a smile and shrugged her shoulders, still staring ahead. "Every time I look at Minstrel I see my dad, pushing me to be the best all the time. It's not good enough to just have fun with a riding school pony, I've got to showjump, become a winner. I can't just be me, I've got to be competitive. I've got to be as good as my sister." Sophie hurled a chip towards a group of starlings and threw the rest in the rubbish bin. "It's quite sad really, I even wrote in to an agony aunt column once but they didn't print the letter. I think they thought I was too pathetic."

"So your sister rides?" I prompted, driven by curiosity to find out more.

"No, that's why I took it up, because she didn't want to. Life would be unbearable if she rode. You see, my sister excels at everything. You name it, tennis, hockey, netball, she's on all the teams. Next to Natalie, I'm a complete failure." Sophie sat hunched forward, her shoulders shaking, her long legs awkwardly splayed out. I knew she wanted to cry but was biting it back because I was there. Now she'd started talking it seemed she couldn't stop.

"I've never been sporty before so when I asked to go to riding school Dad was over the moon. Even Mum thought it was great being able to have a riding hat in the back of the car and gymkhana stickers in the window. And then Dad came to watch me and that was it, I went to pieces, and he said I was useless and couldn't possibly ride a donkey like Rocket. He went out and bought Minstrel and started interfering in my life like he always does. He wanted me to go to Horseworld Centre but I like it here. At Brook House nobody is particularly good at anything, everybody is just ordinary and loves horses, warts and all, for what they are. I belong here more than I do in my own home. You see, Jodie, my dad doesn't love me, he never has done. But it doesn't bother me any more, because I've learnt to live with it. And now I've got Rocket."

A huge lump formed in my throat. I hardly knew what to say. My parents had always been so brilliant and supportive. I couldn't imagine what it must be like to feel as isolated as Sophie. I reached out and held her hand, squeezing reassuringly. The tears had started to spill down her cheeks.

"You know," I started in a whisper, "at my old riding school we had a special pact that everybody

43

had to help each other, so that nobody ever felt alone or unsure. It really helped me when I had to go through some bad things." I hesitated and then went on, "I think the Six Pack should have a rule that we're always there for each other. No matter what."

"I think that's a very good idea." Sophie's fingers clasped mine, gripping tight. "I'm so pleased you came to Brook House, Jodie, because somehow now I think everything's going to be all right." She shuddered slightly and a crooked smile tugged at the corners of her mouth.

And for the first time in two years I realized I wasn't the only twelve-year-old girl to have problems. A huge chunk of bitterness melted into nothing.

"Bending, ride and run, mug, potato, sack, musical sticks . . ."

"Well you'd better cross out Archie for the potato race," said Kate, glancing over Emma's list. "Last year he ate all the potatoes and that's before the races even started."

Sophie and I slipped into the saloon looking sheepish.

"Where've you been?" Emma immediately rounded on us, as if we'd deliberately left her out. "Oh I nearly forgot," she cried, nudging Kate so hard her biro flipped off the page, "put Buz down for the flag race – he's utterly, incredibly ace at it."

"Don't tell me, you've trained him to pick up the flags with his teeth?" Steph teased as she walked in carrying her lunch box and a Wagon Wheel.

"Ha ha, not quite." Emma stuck out her tongue.

"Well, nobody can beat Monty at bending," Steph boasted. "He's a whirlwind."

"Um, I thought we were going to clean out the tack room?" Everybody ignored me and carried on with their gymkhana-mania. "If we don't do the cleaning up, Mrs Brentford won't let us ride the ponies." I tried to load my voice with warning.

"Oh lighten up, Jodie, we'll only be an hour. Then we can start your precious cleaning operation."

"Rachel's gone to tack up Rusty for you," said Kate, giving me a sly glance and watching my expression like a hawk. "If you can't ride at all we can always put you on the lead rein."

"She doesn't have to do anything she doesn't want to do." Sophie immediately leapt to my side.

"Oh for heaven's sake, she doesn't need a nanny," Kate snapped, pressing down her riding hat. "Now are we going to get started or wait until Christmas?"

This was the second time the ponies had been out that day which was nothing for riding school ponies, but they were all bad-tempered and lethargic, swishing at flies and trying to drag their heads down to tug at grass.

45

Rachel led out Blossom who was blowing herself out so her girth wouldn't meet – a common trick with ponies. Rachel was very pale; she was breathing heavily and looked frightened. I knew for a fact that she'd only ever ridden Rusty, and Blossom's rolling, wickedly naughty eyes were scaring her to death.

"It's OK," I said, taking Blossom's reins and turning her back round. "I'm not riding, so you can have Rusty."

Kate, who was just about to mount Archie, did a quick double take and flipped her foot out of the near stirrup. Archie, taking advantage of the situation, sidled into Buzby who, knocked off balance, stood on Emma's toe.

"What do you mean, you're not riding?"

"In case you'd forgotten," I said, glaring back at her with equal venom, "it was only yesterday that I hurt my ankle. You wouldn't want me to drop any more saddles now, would you?"

Kate's eyes swooped down to my jodphur boot as if looking for evidence of swelling. "Well, it's funny," she grunted, tugging Archie's head away from a flower basket, "you've not had a hint of a limp all day."

# Chapter Five

"Three, two, one . . . *Go!*"

Monty did a half rear and shot off and Buzby stared blankly, then crashed into the first bending pole.

"Kick him on!" Kate shouted to Emma who was making futile attempts to neck-rein with her hands sticking out to the side.

Monty whizzed down the line of poles weaving in and out, but completely failed to stop, sailing on for two laps of the field before finally pulling up with Steph perched painfully on the pommel of the saddle, her riding hat slammed down over her nose.

"Wonderful control," Kate sneered, then gave Steph a lecture about flapping her legs even though her own arms were poking about like knitting needles.

"I don't think I can do this," Rachel whispered, leading Rusty across, who was neighing frantically to Ebony Jane in the adjoining field. Her hands were shaking so much she couldn't pull on her special pimple gloves.

"If you knock a pole down you're eliminated,"

Steph shouted to Emma who had jumped off and was readjusting Buzby's noseband.

Rachel stared ahead, overwhelmed with black despair.

"Just take your time," I whispered, trying to instil her with confidence. "As you approach the last pole on your way up the course, go slightly wide so you can make a tight turn. Sit up and use your seat to drive him round."

Kate flew down the course, racing Steph, leaning catlike over Archie's stubby neck and brushing the last pole with hardly an inch to spare.

"Don't let her get to you," I urged, giving Rachel a leg-up. "You can't be expected to ride like that. You're just a novice." Rachel smiled weakly and gathered up the reins.

"I'll give you a head start," Kate shouted to Rachel.

Rusty walked slowly down to the poles, not batting an eyelid.

"Do you think she's all right?" Emma whispered. "I mean, she's only had a few lessons." Rusty's ears cocked back and forth taking in the line of poles. Steph did the start. "Get ready, get set . . . Go!"

Archie bounded forward, his eyes rolling gleefully as he whipped round the first pole.

Rusty broke into a steady trot, lifting his head up to tip Rachel back in the saddle when she fell forward.

48

"Isn't he a sweetheart?" Sophie clasped her hands together and started cheering.

Unfortunately Rusty came to a grinding halt at the last pole, unsure exactly what Rachel wanted. Keeping her cool she gently patted him on the neck and opened her right rein.

"Good boy, Rusty!" Emma shouted hoarsely. Archie, on hearing the shouting, set off in a volley of bucks, imitating a wild bronco, crashed chest first through the last pea cane and galloped three times round a horse chestnut tree before depositing Kate near a clump of thistles.

"Oh dear," Emma giggled, burying her head in Buzby's mane. Kate blushed scarlet and dragged a delighted Archie back to the other ponies. Sophie stuggled to control her facial muscles but began to giggle when a huge rip in Kate's jods came into view, exposing sky-blue knickers.

"Well done, Rachel," I patted Rusty's neck, keen to take the spotlight off Kate.

"What about the mug race?" Sophie piped up, patiently holding Rocket who hadn't had a go yet.

"I'll take you on," Kate snarled, practically grinding her teeth together. Archie was still blowing so Steph suggested she rode Monty.

"Well, it takes two mugs to make a race," teased Sophie, flicking back her long hair into a pink scrunchy. We all knew Kate was determined to win.

The mug race was more complicated and

demanded a lot of skill. Three mugs are placed on the centre three poles in a line of five. Riders race to the furthest mug, grab it and place it on the next pole up. They then return to the middle pole, grabbing the mug and moving it one pole up. Finally they transfer the first mug to the middle pole before racing home.

Emma picked up the plastic cups taken from thermos flasks and placed them on the poles. It was important not to use anything that could smash and hurt the horses.

The air was prickly with tension. Monty side-stepped and fidgeted as Kate lengthened the stirrups. Rocket stood waiting for the slightest leg aid from Sophie. He always wore a leather neck-strap which riders could grab hold of if they lost their balance.

"When you're ready . . ." Steph moved into position for the countdown, still holding Archie. Monty stepped up, sniffing the air excitedly, sweat trickling down his grey neck. Emma and Rachel moved closer to me; Buzby and Rusty were more interested in cramming their mouths with grass.

Kate stared at the line of poles.

"On your marks. Get set. *Go!*"

They shot off, burning down the lines, necks outstretched, one chestnut, one grey, nose to nose. Both girls grabbed the furthest mug and turned neck and neck.

"Come on, Sophie!" Emma yelled, both her hands round her mouth. Rocket was doing everything she asked of him and moved slightly ahead. Sophie grabbed the next mug first. The ground rattled with hollow hoof beats.

"The middle pole!" Emma bawled, even though she wasn't supposed to offer help. Sophie snatched the mug and kicked Rocket on from a standstill into a gallop. Monty was in full flight, bursting up to the first pole, taking advantage of Sophie's few moments of hesitation.

"There's nothing in it," I murmured, gripped with the excitement despite myself. Rachel was clinging on to my arm, squeezing tighter and tighter. "Come on, Sophie – go for it!"

Kate grabbed the last mug at lightning speed. One minute her hand was round it, next minute it flipped up into the air, spinning and then hurtling towards Monty's feet, skimming softly through the long grass. Monty was spooked and ran backwards, threatening to rear. His running martingale tightened but didn't deter him.

"You've got to get off and pick it up!" Emma shrieked, knowing the rules off by heart.

Kate leapt off and ran towards the mug, dragging Monty behind her. But he was having none of it. As soon as she tried to get back on, he went crazy. Kate couldn't even get within three feet of the stirrup. He swirled round and round in tight circles and the harder she pulled on the reins the faster he went.

Sophie flew past the finish line, punching the air with her right arm. Rachel started jumping up and down and ran across to kiss Rocket on the nose.

"You stupid, useless pony." Kate, boiling mad, flung Monty's reins at Steph. "You try and control the idiot," she yelled, "he's your pony." Bright pink spots of humiliation glowed on her cheeks. "These gymkhana games are a complete waste of time."

"Try telling that to Mary King," said Emma, "she's now a champion eventer."

Kate glared at us and then flounced off back to the stables, the rip in her jods getting larger with every stride.

"There goes the Incredible Sulk," said Emma as soon as Kate was out of earshot.

"Well, now we've got rid of the big bad wolf," Rachel said, perking up and shedding some of her shyness, "does anyone fancy taking me on at the flag race?"

I spent an hour in Minstrel's field trying to get him to accept me. All he did was pace relentlessly up and down the side of the thorn hedge, his hind hooves clicking into his front ones as his energy bubbled over. He didn't want anything to do with me. Despite my offerings of carrots, mints and horse nuts, he stuck his head in the air and trotted off, his expression distant and aloof. It was almost as if he'd decided he didn't want anything to do with human beings.

It didn't take me long to realize that he'd probably been watching the gymkhana games from a gap in the hedge. The ground was kicked up to dust and fresh droppings were trodden into the bare earth. Horses are just like people, and my guess was that Minstrel was jealous and felt snubbed and left out. I could hardly blame him. All he'd seen for three months was the four sides of his boring field.

Poor, poor Minstrel. "Come on, boy, you've got to snap out of it. If you don't learn to trust someone soon, heaven knows where you'll end up." I sprawled aimlessly on the grass, sprinkling the horse nuts I'd used to tempt him onto a patch of soil. Defeated.

Minstrel stood at a safe distance, suspicious, his ears flicking back and forth, but interested enough to keep watching. His mane was so long the breeze lifted it up. He had the classic Arab dished head and flared nostrils and his tail fanned out over his back, highlights bleached in from the sun. He was perfect. Outstanding. But I still couldn't ride him. There was a raging war going on in my head. One voice egged me on, and I felt the thrill of sitting on that broad chestnut back. The other filled me with panic. What if the same thing happened again? What if I couldn't do it? What if my leg wasn't strong enough? Raw fear washed over me.

Minstrel snorted, and went hurtling off towards the far corner, revelling in his own power and speed. "Show off," I said, picking up the horse nuts and hurling them towards a clump of grass.

A crazy horse and a girl with a smashed leg and no courage. What a winning pair. The only thing Minstrel and I had in common was our hang-ups. And that wasn't nearly enough to win at the Brook House Annual Open Show. Even if Sophie did give me permission to ride him.

# Chapter Six

"You're late!" Emma shouted, bounding down the drive the next morning with a streak of white emulsion drying on her cheek, clutching a paintbrush. "We've got tons done already, you wouldn't believe it." She bustled me into the yard where Steph was plunging Ebony Jane's black tail into a bucket of hot water. Half the contents of the tack room was sprawled out on the concrete, including all the saddles and a pile of numnahs a foot high.

"Hey, watch out," shrieked Emma, as Steph swirled Ebony's tail round and round to shake off excess water.

Archie was tied up by the next stable with strange pink rollers in his mane and Tinky, the little black Shetland, was wandering loose, treading on various items of tack and raiding someone's lunch box. "We're having a pamper day, you know, brush and go," she giggled, "and we're determined to have the tack room decorated and spick and span by tonight."

Sophie came out of the saloon carrying a dustpan and brush and a pair of rubber gloves. Kate was knocking dust out of some old horse blankets and disturbing all sorts of creepy crawlies.

"Next!" Steph shouted. Emma quickly led Ebony Jane into her stable and Rachel appeared with Blossom, tying her up to the metal ring with a quick release knot. It was just like a conveyor belt. They were even using proper horse shampoo.

"This is amazing," I said, still slightly suspicious. "Is this really the same group of girls who were clawing each other's eyes out yesterday?"

"No, we've been replaced by alien androids." Emma hooted at her own joke.

"Come on, Emma, we need some more hot water." Steph threw a dripping wet sponge at Emma and caught her on the back of the neck.

Just as Emma turned on the outside tap, Kate happened to be walking across the yard and got caught in the line of fire. Unfortunately the jet of water from the hosepipe drenched her expensive new suede boots.

"You pig!" she screeched in an alarmingly extra-terrestrial voice. The scene that followed was complete mayhem. Kate ran forward and grabbed the hosepipe, flicking it up and hitting Emma with a jet straight in her face. Emma screamed and Blossom pulled back on her head collar, snapping the strap, and hurtled off in the direction of the main gate. Steph and Sophie were after her in a shot which left Emma, Rachel, Kate and me to face a furious Mrs Brentford.

It wouldn't have been so bad if the yard hadn't been an absolute tip.

"This isn't good enough, girls!" She walked stiffly across to the tap and turned off the gushing water, still flooding out of the hosepipe. "I want all this cleared up by the time I get back from golf this afternoon. Lift your game, girls, otherwise you'll all be out on your ear. Is that clear?" There was no doubt she meant it. I knew she felt I'd let her down.

"She is such a hypocrite!" Kate let rip as soon as we were alone. "She sticks her head in the sand and refuses to acknowledge that the riding school is in trouble. At least we're trying to do something about it. All she's doing is running away." I had to admit that, for the first time since I'd met her, Kate did have a point.

"So where's Blossom?" Emma asked in a deadpan voice.

"That's the million dollar question," said Rachel staring down the drive. "So where exactly do we start looking?"

Blossom was in her element, haring round the next door neighbour's vegetable patch, her fat little belly brushing the rows of sweet peas. Sophie and Steph were scarlet and out of breath. Every time they got close she slipped out of range. Eventually we got her cornered and she shot under the runner beans and hid under the foliage, trying to look innocent.

"At least we know what class to enter her for at the show," panted Emma, resting her hands on her knees. Blossom pulled at a runner bean. "Most Appealing Pony."

"She'll have to appeal to somebody's better nature when this lot gets discovered," said Sophie as she dragged her out like a tugboat, "otherwise we're well and truly done for."

"God, it's hot," Sophie lay on the grass, running an ice cube over her forehead and cheeks. The tack room was like a furnace and we were taking it in turns to do the painting. Everybody was in shorts and crop tops – I was the only one sweltering in stretch jeans and a baggy T-shirt. The dull, thrumming ache had started up in my leg. Any extremes of temperature always set it off, and stupidly, I'd left my painkillers at home on the kitchen sink.

I'd caught the early bus that morning and sneaked round to the back fields before anyone arrived to spend an hour with Minstrel, trying to coax him to come to me. I sat in the middle of the field pretending to read a book and he'd eventually come over and started sniffing my hair, curious to see what I was doing. It had felt like a real breakthrough. Minstrel loved being the centre of attention and ignoring him seemed the best way of getting him to do what I wanted. After endless patience I had managed to slip on a head collar and lead him up and down. He was even more brilliant than I had imagined. He just seemed to float through the air.

"Jodie?" Sophie's voice brought me back to reality. She was staring at my legs. "Why don't you put some shorts on?"

"I'm OK, I don't wear shorts," I replied.

Emma sat up, fanning herself with a dock leaf, her face bright pink from the sun. Sophie rummaged in her rucksack, spilling out deodorant, hoof pick, mane comb and fly repellent. "Don't be daft," she said, "everybody wears shorts. Here – I knew I'd brought a spare pair." To my horror she whipped out a pair of crumpled Union Jack knee-length shorts and tossed them over so they half-fell in my lap. I was frozen rigid with panic.

"I don't want them." I brushed them off, suddenly feeling cold and sick. Sophie flinched, obviously hurt. For a moment no one said anything, no one moved. "Just leave it, all right? You don't understand, nobody does." I leapt up, too fast, twanging my leg, emotions rioting inside me. I was making a complete fool of myself but I didn't know what else to do. I couldn't handle it. I couldn't handle my life.

"Jodie?"

I stumbled off towards the stables, tripping over

the hosepipe, cannoning into Rusty's stable door. Why did I overreact like this? Why couldn't I just tell people the truth and be done with it?

I headed towards the saloon wanting a few minutes to myself before I went back to apologize to Sophie. I could hear raised voices before I even got to the louvred doors. I paused, rocking on my heels, unsure what to do next. The voices belonged to Kate and Rachel, I was sure of it. I thought about sneaking past but Kate's voice was so clear I couldn't help overhearing. I hovered uncertainly, feeling compelled to listen, and peered through the crack in the door.

Kate was going for the jugular. "Don't you ever humiliate me like that again," she hissed. "I'm the one who runs things round here, not Jodie. And next time we do gymkhana races, don't make me look a fool."

Rachel said something which I couldn't quite hear.

"Just remember what I know," said Kate. "One word from me and you'll never see Brook House again. And then what will happen to your precious little Rusty?"

Rachel blanched and recoiled, stepping back against the table. My breath caught in my throat. Kate was not only bossy and a bad loser she was something far worse – a bully. And whatever dark secret she knew about Rachel was having a devastating effect. Poor Rachel looked utterly terrified.

I didn't have time to think. Suddenly Kate was walking towards the door. I pressed up against the wall, my heart beating furiously. She marched out, stomping across to the tack room without even a backward glance. I'd escaped from being caught by the skin of my teeth. But I had to act quickly – before my luck ran out. If Kate looked back now she'd know I'd been listening. I dived into the saloon because it was the only place available. Rachel was gasping for breath.

"Rachel!" Fear rose up inside me. I'd never seen anybody like this. "Rachel, what is it? What can I do?" I held her shoulders. Frantically she pointed towards a blue sports bag slung in the corner.

"Look Jodie, I'm really sorry if I upset . . ." Sophie crashed through the louvred doors, head down, intent on getting out what she had to say. As soon as she saw Rachel she stopped dead in her tracks. "Oh no!" She belted across to the blue bag, turned it upside down and rummaged around.

"Here!" Sophie thrust something into Rachel's hand. An inhaler. Rachel sucked in deep hungry breaths, her eyes relaxing as the colour slowly trickled back into her cheeks. Relief surged through me. She was going to be all right. Sophie kept a comforting arm round her shoulders as her breathing gradually righted itself, the wheezing subsiding.

Rachel gave me a lopsided, guilty grin and sat down on one of the plastic chairs. Even now she looked pale and exhausted.

"She has asthma." Sophie tried to be matter of fact. "Something usually sets it off." She cocked an eyebrow at Rachel, speculative, thoughtful. "I wonder what it could have been?"

# Chapter Seven

"Paint fumes, definitely," said Rachel nodding, trying to convince herself as we both tacked up Rusty. I decided not to mention what I'd overheard to anyone, not until I'd had time to sleep on it. I didn't want to cause more trouble for Rachel.

Rusty gently nudged my back insisting that I carry on brushing his face. He was quite bony round the eyes so I used a soft water brush and dabbed it under his forelock. Not many ponies liked their faces being brushed, but Rusty loved it. He was a strawberry roan which meant that his coat was a mixture of white, red and black hairs. He wore a simple snaffle bridle which was one of the mildest types of bit, unlike Archie and Buzby who wore kimblewicks because the bars or gums of their mouths had gone hard from too much rough handling. Most riding school ponies were dead to the hand and leg, because of novice riders. In some ways they were a real challenge but usually responded to a good rider. Rusty was just an angel and tried to please everybody.

"True or false?" Emma appeared over the stable

door, holding the latest edition of *In the Saddle*. "A family of greater crested newts lives in the water jump at Hickstead and have to be moved every year before the Derby."

"That's not fair," I said. "It's supposed to be off the top of your head, not from a magazine." Emma and I were having a true or false competition and up to now Emma hadn't got a single point.

Rachel and I carried on brushing Rusty.

"Sandra says the diary's nearly full for next week and guess what?" Emma pouted her lips, desperate to tell. "The new instructor's going to be starting too." We were suddenly interested. "That's all I know," she added, putting an end to the suspense. "I hope she's like Zoe Ball."

"Oh no, Mary King," said Rachel, "She's so nice."

"Just as long as she's not a replica of Janice," I added, "otherwise there'll be no riding school left to worry about."

"Oh, and about the newts, it was true," called Emma as she ran off. "One point to me."

The tack room was finished by three o'clock so we had the rest of the afternoon to school the ponies. It looked a million times better by anyone's standards. We'd even pinned up posters of different breeds of ponies over the cracks in the walls.

We led the ponies into the manege, Archie, Buzby

and Rusty. The air was humid and full of midges, and Rocket tried to rub his tail on one of the fence posts. Rachel clambered onto Rusty, seemingly OK, although Sophie and I were watching over her like hawks.

The manege was a rectangle filled with sand, with a jumping lane down one side. There was a line of three jumps already at a height of two foot six, the last one being a spread with a little red and white filler at the front. Buzby eyed it dubiously and skitted across the arena, pulling at the reins which slid through Emma's hands.

Kate was already on Archie, circling him at the far end and trying to get him to do a square halt. That is when all four hooves halt together. To do this you have to squeeze with your hands, sit up and keep your legs on. In any downward transition such as trot to walk or walk to halt, it is really important to hold the horse together with your legs every stride.

Sophie mounted Rocket, making sure she hopped round and didn't jab him in the ribs with her toe. Rachel suggested doing some exercises and started touching her toes and doing half scissors.

"That's baby stuff," taunted Steph as she marched in, clutching a can of Coke and dragging Monty who wasn't looking very cooperative.

"In case you've forgotten, Rachel's a beginner." Sophie rolled her eyes in annoyance.

"Oh crikey, Kate's already started." Steph, not hearing, dumped the Coke and her sweatshirt in my arms and frantically tightened the girth. "Kate's invited me to her farm in Cornwall for two weeks," she couldn't help boasting. "We're going to ride proper thoroughbred horses."

"Oh, bully for you," Emma mocked, "Nice to know that Kate's got a new lapdog at last."

"I'll ignore that comment," Steph bristled, pursing her lips. "Jealousy doesn't become you, Emma, you should know better." She stuck her nose in the air and rode off with her elbows flapping.

"Well, she's got as much chance of going to Cornwall as I have of going to planet Mars." Emma wrinkled her nose.

"How do you know that?" I looked up.

"Because," said Emma, wagging a finger, "we've all been invited to precious Cornwall at some stage over the last year, haven't we, Soph? And never mind thoroughbred horses, we haven't even seen as much as a Cornish pasty."

"It's a schooling programme!" I explained in exasperation. I handed round the detailed printouts which I'd done on my brother's computer. "It's designed to show up each pony's strengths and weaknesses."

I'd spent all last night programming in each horse and pony's age, temperament and ability, to

66

produce individual worksheets. I'd even done horsy graphics in the corner which looked really cool. I was quite proud of what I'd come up with.

"But according to this we don't have any strengths at all." Emma was referring to Buzby.

"And what exactly is a figure-of-eight-and-a-half halt?" Rachel was nonplussed.

"You're a funny girl, Jodie." Sophie flipped through the pages. "Only you could come up with something as organized as this."

We'd just been practising jumping which Rocket was surprisingly good at. Buzby took off in a kind of helicopter-style and landed on the other side, all four feet clumped together, his head bashing Emma on the nose. Rachel wisely decided to stick to flat-work and I helped her with rising trot and changing diagonals. Kate, so far, had ignored us which was fine by me. Steph decided to jump Monty and promptly demolished the whole jumping lane.

"What about you, Kate?" Sophie shouted across, a slight challenge rising in her voice.

"Archie doesn't jump," Kate shouted back, her voice flat and dismissive.

"But every pony jumps," Emma argued. "Even Buzby. Don't tell me you're scared."

It wasn't meant to be a criticism. I think it just popped out as a joke. But even so, it struck a raw nerve. Kate rode across looking black with rage.

Suddenly the air hung heavy with tension.

Nobody spoke. Kate's mouth disappeared into a tight line. "I really don't think I'm the one you should be accusing of being scared." She glared straight at me with bullet-hard eyes. "As Jodie obviously knows so much about riding I think she should be the one to jump Archie, don't you?"

Steph's face lit up as she sensed trouble. Sophie's mouth dropped open in panic. It was almost as if I knew this was going to happen. As if I wanted someone to put me on the spot, push me into a corner. Make the decision for me.

"I'll ride," I blurted out, my heart hammering. "But not Archie." It was now or never. I could hardly hold my voice steady. I glanced at Sophie for support, resolve strengthening inside me. "If it's all right with you, Soph," I stammered, turning my gaze to Kate, adrenalin pumping through my body, "I'll ride Minstrel."

"He'll kill you!" Sophie ran after me, white with fear, as I headed for Minstrel's field. "This is crazy, you can't ride."

For once Emma didn't have anything to say. Kate immediately backed off, arguing that I was taking the dare too far. There was no sign of Mrs Brentford at the house.

"*Jodie, stop it!*" Sophie refused to let me pass, so I ducked under her arm.

"She's bluffing," Steph said, not at all sure.

I'd never felt more certain of anything in my whole life.

"What if Rocket's saddle doesn't fit?" Sophie tried a new angle.

"Then I'll fetch another one that does." I marched on, determined, concentrating on taking level strides, making each leg work as if nothing had ever happened.

Minstrel charged up to the gate, snorting. On guard as six girls headed towards him.

"I don't want anyone else to go in the field." My voice shook.

"Fine," Steph snapped. "It's your funeral." Rachel, Sophie and Emma glared at her with maximum venom.

"You don't have to do this," Kate said, crumbling slightly.

Minstrel tore up the field at a gallop, then came trotting back, tossing his beautiful copper-red head and showing off with a few extended strides.

"Crikey," Rachel gulped. "He's enormous."

"Whoa boy, steady now, there's my little beauty," I coaxed and tried to hide the frantic pelting of my heart as I ran a hand over the massive crested neck which could only belong to a stallion. Minstrel stamped at some flies, each vein on his chest and flanks pulsing under the surface with barely contained energy. I stood stock-still and let him sniff

69

over the saddle, squealing and thrashing about as he picked up the scent of another horse.

"Please God, let him be safe," I said to myself, crossing my fingers for a second, then easing the saddle and numnah onto the broad, powerful back. Minstrel quivered but didn't move. He only tensed as I tightened the girth, gently pulling on the buckle. It was almost as if he was eager to get on with the job. I moved round to the right-hand side, readjusting Sophie's riding hat and easing down the stirrup. Minstrel was a good hand bigger than anything I'd ever ridden before. His withers seemed to be stuck up in another galaxy.

"I don't believe this," Kate cut in, breaking my concentration, "She's getting on on the wrong side." Minstrel sidestepped away from my foot, his trust in me suddenly subsiding. Rachel's eyes grew like saucers, shocked at my lack of basic knowledge.

For a second I felt like giving in. Then Kate's cold sneer lodged in my brain like an irritating wasp. I had something to prove.

"I'll give you a leg-up." Sophie hopped over the fence. My left leg would never have stood the strain of getting on from the correct side. My physiotherapist had already informed me of that. Minstrel allowed Sophie to approach, watching warily as she bent down to support my leg.

"After three," she mumbled.

I gathered up the reins, relishing the feel of soft leather between my fingers.

"Three, two, one – up."

I eased my leg over Minstrel's back, settling into the saddle. I could barely breathe for nerves. Minstrel immediately hunched and flattened his ears. "It's all right, boy, I'm not going to hurt you."

The heat coming through his burning skin reminded me that it was all new for him too. We were both feeling our way. I closed my eyes and pushed him forward. The strength and power were unbelievable. He just seemed to devour the ground with massive long strides.

"Hold steady, hold steady," I murmured to myself, trying to keep my hands as light as possible and mould my left leg round his side. Minstrel snorted and launched forward like no other horse I'd ever been on. He just seemed to float through the air, his hooves not touching the ground. Every other pony I'd ridden had a definite thud. Minstrel was in a class of his own. I probably relaxed too early. I released the pressure on the reins just a little, so he could stretch forward and shift into canter. I was going through a mental checklist – shoulders back, hands still, elbows in, chin up, but my heart was soaring. Hot, emotional tears trickled down my cheeks and into the chin guard of Sophie's riding hat. It was really happening. I was back in the saddle.

Minstrel bounded forward, swishing through the thick grass, leaning into the bridle. His canter was so smooth I hardly moved in the saddle. We were gelling completely when suddenly Frank's huge head poked through the hedge taking us both by surprise. Minstrel slammed on the brakes. Frank's enormous ears wafted back and forth as he pushed harder against the fence. I tilted forwards and lost my left stirrup.

We would have been all right if, in an effort to keep on top, I hadn't accidentally jabbed Minstrel in the mouth. It was only a tweak but it sent him absolutely berserk. Throwing back his head, he lunged forward, hurling the reins loose and bunching up for an almighty buck. I clamped my knees tight on the saddle flaps and shut my eyes.

"Jodie!" Sophie's stricken voice rent the air.

The bucks came fast and varied, Minstrel contorting himself into every position possible. I'd never felt anything like it. He set off on a diagonal across the field, arching his back and lifting all four feet off the ground at once like a bronco. The secret was to get his head up and push him out of it, but I didn't dare put any pressure on the reins in case he flipped completely.

My eyes were a blur of tears. A branch switched across my cheek as we hurtled under some low lying trees. It was like being stuck on the worst ride at Alton Towers. "I don't know what to do," I

72

mumbled, flinging my arms round Minstrel's neck. "Oh please stop, *please*!"

For a few seconds Minstrel galloped even faster, still trying to shake me off like an annoying fly. He was all bucked out now and the fun seemed to have gone out of his game. I caught a glimpse of the five girls, staring with wild panic, horror-stricken. I grinned and tried to look as if I knew what I was doing.

Suddenly, with no warning, Minstrel dropped into trot and then into walk, his ears back, ready to listen to me. The tension just seemed to flood out of his body and he moved forward as if in a dressage test. The whirlwind had passed. I patted his neck, laughing and crying at the same time. "Good boy, clever boy." I buried my face in his silky red mane and patted his shoulder. Gently I neck-reined him back to the gate, trembling like crazy, but mostly with elation.

"How on earth did you manage to stay on?" Emma was looking at me with new respect. Even Steph didn't have any snide remark.

Sophie turned away quickly, trying to hide the hurt that was written all over her face. "You never told us that you could ride."

I slithered down from Minstrel who was relishing all the attention, rubbing his nose on my arm, not letting me move a centimetre away from him.

It was now or never. Bending down, I slowly

rolled up the bottom of my jean jods, tugging the material higher and higher until it exposed the mangled left calf with its criss-crosses of purple-blue scars and a dent the size of a fifty pence piece.

"I had a riding accident." My voice faltered. "I was fooling around on the roads and my pony slipped and rolled on top of me. It was all my fault. I broke my leg in seven places and severed some nerves. I didn't tell you because I was ashamed and angry, and, well, I was scared. It was easier just to let you believe I couldn't ride."

For a moment, all the girls were lost for words.

"We didn't know," Steph ventured at last.

"How could you?" I gulped back a wave of emotion. "This is the first time I've told anyone."

Kate suddenly turned and walked off without saying a word.

"What's eating her?" Emma stared after her.

"That must have taken so much courage," Sophie said in a half whisper.

And then my face crumpled with relief and emotion and I hugged Minstrel's neck, burying my face in his mane, thanking him over and over again for giving me back something so special – my confidence.

# Chapter Eight

The next few days at Brook House were fantastic. It was as if by riding Minstrel I'd passed some sort of special initiation ceremony. All the girls worked like slaves to get the stables, feed room and saloon looking immaculate. Every horse and pony received a make-over, a bath, a mane and tail pull and a feathers and ears trim. We didn't touch their whiskers because horses use them as feelers and it isn't right to cut them off.

Kate was unusually quiet and poured all her energies into launching the Brook House Young Riders Club and producing the first newsletter which Sophie promised to copy on her dad's photocopier. There were profiles on three of the riding school ponies, Buzby, Rocket and Rusty, their likes, dislikes, personalities, breeds, and tips on how best to ride them and also on grooming and stable management. Kate asked me to produce a special helpline page which I secretly thought was a brilliant idea, and I concentrated on articles with headlines like, "Too Scared to Jump" and "I Can't Stop!", offering riding tips, quotes and personal experiences from various riders at the school. Kate did a star profile on the new riding instructor, getting all the information from Mrs Brentford but refusing to show it to anyone.

"That girl is so annoying." Sophie threw herself onto the new settee in the saloon which had been donated by Emma's parents. "Why does she always have to be queen bee?"

Apart from bragging about her horsy uncle in Hong Kong and pretending she knew everything about Arabs, Kate hadn't caused any more trouble. Rachel refused to open up to me about the argument they'd had and just stayed out of her way. In fact, since I'd ridden Minstrel, Rachel had elevated me to hero worship status. Nobody mentioned the accident, which was just as well because I didn't want to go on and on about it. Everybody was really understanding though and even Kate showed a grudging admiration.

I spent every spare minute with Minstrel, talking to him, handling him and schooling him on the manege in between lessons. Sophie was thrilled to bits that he was going so well but showed no inclination to try him out herself. On the inside of the saloon door Steph had pinned up a list of some of the ponies with the events they should be entered for at the Brook House Show next to their names.

ROCKET: *Novice jumping – 14.2hh and under. Best ridden.*
BUZBY: *Most appealing pony? Flag race, potato, minimus, fancy dress.*
RUSTY: *Best turned out. Veteran pony. Bending, mug, minimus.*
ARCHIE: *Best ridden. Definitely no jumping.*
BLOSSOM: *Best riding school pony. Most appealing pony. (Someone apologize to next-door neighbour for garden.)*
MONTY: *Everything.*

I was itching to add Minstrel's name for the open jumping in the 14.2hh and under category. Yesterday, I'd secretly tried him over an upright and a spread and he'd been nothing short of brilliant.

"He's fantastic!" Emma blasted into the saloon, dark blond hair flopping round her face. She was slightly out of breath, her lips parted. "Carl Hester eat your heart out, they'll be flocking here in droves. We'll be the biggest riding school in the country. Buzby could become a cult figure."

Steph and Rachel were too busy playing with a Cyberpet to take much notice. Kate was applying some denim-coloured nail varnish which was supposed to be the latest craze and didn't even look up.

"Excuse me?" I interrupted Emma in mid-flow. "What exactly are you talking about?"

Kate stood up, trying to look as bored as possible.

"I think she's referring to the new temporary riding instructor," she said dismissively. "His name's Guy Marshall and he's a showjumper. He's on the arena right now. Oh, and he's invited me round to see his horses which I thought was rather sweet."

"I just can't take it in." Sophie stuck her feet forward on Rocket and fiddled with the stirrups. "Pinch me hard someone, quick! Two years at riding school and we've finally got a good instructor!"

Guy was absolutely drop-dead gorgeous with soft brown eyes and unruly blond hair. He couldn't have been more than twenty-seven years old and, even better, he was a superb instructor. The riding school had never been so busy. Within a week Mrs Brentford had to start doing evening lessons to fit everyone in. Ebony Jane and Frank were brought out of semi-retirement and Guy even started breaking in Elvis and Faldo who thought it was great to be part of the team. The whole place was buzzing. Even pupils who had just been walking and trotting for months progressed to canter and jumping.

Guy insisted on discipline and told Steph off twice for getting too close to Rachel in our group lesson, telling her that next time she'd have to leave the arena. Emma didn't gossip once and even Buzby decided to behave and kept giving Guy respectful glances, especially after he'd been chased down the long side with the lunge whip.

Within no time Guy had Rachel doing rising trot properly. He started her off by showing her how to roll out of the saddle in walk. Novices tended to shoot up too high in the saddle when really all you have to do is follow the horse's movement. After half an hour doing sitting trot she could rise out of the saddle in rhythm.

Minstrel hated being in a group lesson so I'd had twenty minutes on my own with Guy earlier. He'd said that Minstrel could go right to the very top and was really impressed with my jumping position. However I had to learn not to fold my upper body before take-off and to leave Minstrel alone in the last three strides. Guy said the rider's job was to keep the horse balanced, in rhythm at the right speed, and going straight. I'd never learnt so much in so short a time. The secret to jumping a course was to think and look ahead, choosing exactly the right line to each fence. Minstrel tended to buck after each jump and I had to sit up and drive him forward. Guy showed me how to use my left seat bone and thigh to compensate for the weakness in my calf.

Buzby was rapidly running out of tricks when Guy showed Emma how to stop him squashing her leg against the surrounding fence. All she had to do was use more outside leg and inside rein to push him away and if that didn't work she had to give him a short sharp smack down the outside shoulder with the riding crop. Buzby immediately mended his ways.

"He's utterly brilliant," Sophie gushed after Rocket had jumped a fence of two foot nine without any hesitation. Once Sophie had learnt to keep her legs wrapped around Rocket's sides on the approach to the jump, she grew and grew in confidence. It was all about technique.

Kate was skulking around the stables with a migraine so Guy suggested I ride Archie in her place. I would never have dreamed of riding him but Guy was really persuasive and Kate was nowhere in sight.

Archie was quite stubby in his neck and shoulder which made his stride short but he had a natural rhythm so he was good at flatwork. Guy asked me to form the rear of the ride and then told us all to ride down the centre line in single file before splitting off in opposite directions when we reached a certain point. The ponies wanted to follow each other, so we had to use lots of leg and ride a straight line to the outside track.

Guy was altering the jumping lane to a small fence with a filler and a pole three strides in front to guide the pony in. "OK," he said, shooting me a sizzling, megawatt smile, "let's see Archie in action."

"But he can't jump," I protested. Archie, immediately sensing something different, latched onto Buzby like a magnet.

"I'll decide that," said Guy, raising the pole on the jump a notch higher. "Emma can give you a lead – just keep your legs on and wait for the jump to come to you."

Buzby set off in a stuffy trot, furious that he had to go in the lead. Guy had put some red tape on Emma's reins so she knew exactly where to hold them. She still flapped her elbows but her riding had improved enormously. Archie followed on, swishing his tail and rolling his eyes.

"Think positive, think positive," I said to myself as I turned him into the jumping lane just as Buzby cleared the fence with a flourish. "Come on, Archie, you can do it." I lined him up straight, aiming for the middle of the fence.

"Come on, Archie!" Rachel shouted out from on top of Rusty, not knowing that you had to be quiet.

My whole concentration was focused on the jump. Archie tensed, bracing himself, his eyes wide with shock. I squeezed my legs round his sides and thought hard about clearing the jump. For a few seconds Archie paddled, unsure, his palomino head flicking up. Then he seemed to make up his mind and bounded forward, flying into the air, his forelegs tucked up. He cleared the pole by a foot. I was so taken aback I lost both stirrups and collapsed on his neck.

"Whoopee!" Emma shrieked, insistent that Archie had his eyes closed going over the fence. "He was mega!" I patted him ecstatically and Archie swanked past Buzby, practically grinning with delight. Buzby scowled and tried to nip his shoulder to bring him back down to earth.

"Who said this pony couldn't jump?" Guy cocked an eyebrow at me and tutted under his breath. Sophie caught my gaze; our confusion was mutual. Kate was a really good rider. Why on earth, after two years at Brook House, had she convinced everybody that Archie couldn't jump?

We dismounted and ran up the stirrups ready to go back to the stables. Guy gave us all a rundown of our good and bad points and where we'd improved. Rachel was glowing with happiness and hugging Rusty to death. Guy was the best instructor ever. He inspired everyone with confidence. Back in the yard, the next ride were waiting in the office with Sandra. Sophie reluctantly handed over Rocket to a girl in a bright pink body protector.

I put Archie in his stable with the reins under his stirrups just in case he was being used on the next ride which was a one hour hack. That's when I spotted Kate in Minstrel's stable, beaming from ear to ear. Suddenly, without any real reason, my blood ran cold.

I crossed the yard instinctively knowing that something was wrong. As Kate swivelled round, I saw the Magic Mane Puller clasped in her right hand. She'd been showing off with it all morning – it was a revolutionary trimmer which left manes neatly pulled but in a fraction of the time. Everybody was buying them. The worst thought possible crossed my mind. Surely she wouldn't, couldn't . . . *Oh no, please.*

"There you are!" She opened the stable door wearing her smug, "everything's left to me" smile. "Somebody had to tidy him up, he looked a right mess."

By the water bucket was a huge pile of fine chestnut hair swept into a neat pile. Minstrel whickered and barged for the door, delighted to see me.

"Oh no," I whimpered. His gorgeous long mane was hacked back to five centimetres in length and stuck up on the crest of his neck where it was too short to lie down. Kate waited for praise, oblivious to the harm she'd done.

"Oh dear." Sophie came up behind me.

It was only then that I realized my shoulders were shaking. "You stupid girl." My voice came out as a hoarse whisper. Minstrel backed up a step, his ears twitching. "Everybody knows that Arabs have long manes. Only an idiot would do this." I waved a hand at the cropped hair lying on the floor. "You're the one who's supposed to know everything about Arabs."

Kate rocked back on her heels, flinching at the white-hot anger in my voice. But I didn't care. "Even Rachel wouldn't have made a gaffe like this," I continued, my voice rising.

Somewhere in the back of my mind cogs started rolling, pieces of the jigsaw clicking into place. "But you don't really know anything do you?" I was speaking slowly now, fumbling through the fog to get at the truth. "The uncle in Hong Kong, a farm in Cornwall, an Arab for your fifteenth birthday – it's all lies, nothing but lies. You're just an ordinary girl like me trying to make yourself sound important. You're a cheat, a con."

Kate went pale, tears springing into her eyes. Emma, Rachel and Steph joined Sophie at the door, open-mouthed with shock.

"You even lied about Archie not being able to jump. Don't tell me you're too scared to jump after you've made fun of everybody else?" A crimson flush of embarrassment flooded up Kate's neck.

"God, I'm right, aren't I? You can't help yourself, you're a compulsive liar" Kate pushed past me, scuffing my shoulder. She tore off towards the saloon, stifling a sob, head bowed down.

"All the rubbish we took from her," said Sophie, slowly shaking her head in disbelief. "Why would anyone want to make up stories like that?"

We headed off to the local shop, all five of us, trying to absorb what we'd found out, just needing to get away from the stables. By the time we came back up the drive an hour later, Kate had gone. All that was left of her was a cardboard certificate verifying her as a member of the Six Pack, which had been ripped in half, and the file on the Young Riders Club. The Six Pack had effectively become the Five Pack.

"Good riddance." Emma picked up the torn card and hurled it in the bin.

I helped Guy with evening stables, rubbing down the horses and filling hay nets, lugging water buckets across the yard until my legs were soaked. Minstrel was in particularly high spirits and refused to let me put on his summer rug or pick out his feet. He looked ridiculous with a short mane but there was nothing anybody could do apart from wait until it grew back.

"Neither of us is perfect now." I scratched the top of his withers which he loved and he carefully balanced his chin on my shoulder. All my dreams were tied up with Minstrel. It was almost as if fate had given me a second chance. Somebody had looked down and put a beautiful, talented stallion in my path which nobody wanted. I didn't dream about the accident any more, I dreamt about Minstrel and what we could achieve together.

I saw Sophie heading straight for Minstrel's stable. I could tell immediately that something was wrong. Rocket was waiting impatiently for his food but Sophie didn't even look across when he banged at his door. She was totally absorbed in something else.

"Um, can I have a word?" She bit down on her lip, twiddling nervously with a toggle on her fleece sweatshirt. "I talked to my dad last night," she said, looking away, searching for the right words. I knew Sophie well enough to notice she was faintly embarrassed. "He's offered to finance the riding school as a silent partner if I enter Minstrel for the Brook House Show." I stared at her, uncomprehending. "He wants me to ride," she added and stroked Minstrel's cheek, tracing the outline of his jawbone.

I felt as if someone had chucked ice water all over me. "But you can't." I dropped the body brush which made Minstrel run to the back of the stable. "That's emotional blackmail, it's not fair. He's manipulating you. Anyway, the riding school's doing really well."

Something in Sophie's eyes made me break off and a lump formed in my throat. It wasn't just Sophie's dad. Sophie wanted to ride Minstrel. It showed in the sparkle of excitement, the dilated pupils dancing with anxiety and adrenalin. "I think I can do it," she murmured. "I've got so much more confidence now. It's a chance to finally impress

Dad." She raced on, her mind made up. "I can't do it without you, though. You will help me, won't you?" She fixed me with an intense gaze.

I forced back bitter, burning tears and pulled my mouth into a smile. "Of course I will," I whispered. "After all, Minstrel is your horse."

# Chapter Nine

"Are you sure this is legal?" I was crouched behind a Vauxhall Estate, glancing round, terrified that we might be seen. Emma was darting round the car park, flicking photocopied sheets of Kate's profile on Guy under everyone's windscreens. We'd talked Emma's mum into dropping us off at Horseworld Centre on the pretext of visiting their saddlery shop. She didn't suspect a thing.

"Hurry up, can't you?" I hissed, convinced I'd heard footsteps approaching. My heart was hammering.

Emma had come up with the bright idea of poaching Horseworld's customers by sticking Guy's picture on everyone's windscreens. I'd only gone along with it our of sheer curiosity to see the riding school and now my nerves were stretched to breaking point. I'd been irritable and depressed all morning about Sophie riding Minstrel and the last thing I wanted was to get caught red-handed, crouched next to a car wheel. Eventually, after what seemed like hours but must only have been a couple of minutes, I stood up and decided to rescue a stray sheet of paper which had got trapped under a pitchfork. Emma had completely disappeared from sight.

Horseworld Centre wasn't half as smart as I'd imagined. I couldn't help noticing the loose straw in the grates and corners and the scruffy stable doors streaked with dirt. Brook House was now a hundred times better. The only thing that Horseworld Centre had which we didn't, was an indoor school.

"Can I help you?"

I leapt round, twisting my foot in my haste. A tallish man was standing directly behind me, smiling at my discomfort, dressed in jeans and an Iron Maiden T-shirt.

"Um, I, well . . ." I began, and quickly stuffed the crumpled sheet of paper in my pocket. "I was interested in some lessons." It was the only thing I could think of to say. Any minute now, he'd spot the fliers or Emma would come bolting round the corner.

"Oh well, you've come to the right person." A cheery smile was fixed on his face. "I'm the chief instructor." My eyebrows rose with shock. Mrs Brentford always insisted on a shirt and tie and jodhpurs and jacket for instructors. He looked too scruffy to be a qualified teacher.

"Of course it depends what you're interested in.

We do one or two hour hacks, group lessons, or private."

He led me towards the first row of stables where a chestnut pony was staggering about in a stupor. It was obviously in a bad way.

"If you'd just excuse me." The instructor shot off to answer a telephone which was ringing in a nearby office. Relief surged through me in waves. *But where was Emma?*

Suddenly the sliding door of the school scraped back and ponies filed out, automatically heading for their own stables despite having riders on their backs, just like at Brook House. A cluster of mothers chatted while heading for the car park area so I couldn't get across without being noticed.

I was running now, my breath rasping, just wanting to escape. At each stable door I stopped and looked in, desperate to find Emma, but just seeing gorgeous ponies munching at hay nets. They were all so eye-catching and good-looking – not the usual riding school types at all. It was as if they'd been hand-picked for their beauty and nothing else.

A cold prickle of fear ran down my back. Most beginners wanted to ride beautiful highly-bred ponies but it was usually a recipe for disaster. I was shocked when I pushed open the mouth of a bay 13.2. From what I could tell by looking at her teeth, she was only three years old!

"Finally!" Emma's voice hissed behind me.

"Where've you been? Can't you stay in one spot for two minutes?"

"*Me* stay in one spot, what about *you*?" I broke off when I saw the strain in her face. Emma was always so jolly and joking, but this time she looked really worried.

"Take a look at this." She pulled a red and black poster out of her jeans pocket and opened it out. The words leapt out with sickening clarity: Horse-world Show and Gymkhana. Open Jumping and Ridden Classes. Sunday 14th August. Prompt Start.

The same day as the Brook House Show.

"We're really in trouble now." Emma voiced my own whirring thoughts. "This is a cheap trick and they've done it on purpose."

Even worse, the poster advertised local celebrity eventers, Ash Burgess and Alex Johnson as guests of honour. I leaned back against the wooden stable partition feeling sick with disappointment. All the work we'd put in over the last two weeks . . . Who'd want to come to Brook House now?


"We already know." Sophie raised her head out of her hands, her eyes red-rimmed and swollen. She was slumped in the saloon looking thoroughly depressed. "And it gets a whole lot worse, believe me."

"Mrs Brentford's closing down the riding school." Steph walked in behind us, blurting out the

91

devastating news before Sophie had a chance to finish.

"She's selling out to a builder." Sophie's voice caught in her throat. "Rocket's stable is likely to become a retirement bungalow! All the horses are going up for sale. They'll be split up and sent goodness knows where. Dear, sweet ponies like Rusty who's done nothing but try to please all his life. Frank and Ebony Jane, what's going to happen to them? It makes me sick. We can't let it happen."

I moved across to her, putting my arms round her shoulders as she let the tears fall freely.

Emma stood stock-still, unable to speak. Steph raked a hand through her hair and pressed her forehead against the cool glass pane of the window. "Dad will sell Monty for sure now. He's just been trying to find an excuse."

"Could someone find Rachel?" Sophie mopped at her eyes with a crumpled tissue. "She ran off when we told her. I'm worried about her asthma. You know how she feels about Rusty – he's her life, she worships him."

"And what about Buzby?" Emma spoke for the first time in an unnatural voice. "I'd rather kidnap him than let him go to some grotty kid who doesn't understand his special ways. Without Buz there's no point to anything."

"We won't let it happen," I surprised myself with my own determination.

"I appreciate what you're saying, Jodie," Sophie half-smiled, struggling to find strength. "But at the end of the day we're just a bunch of kids. And who's going to listen to us?"

*Dear Rusty,*
*I'll miss you heaps. I'll never forget you and the brill times we had together.*

*Rachel*

The note fluttered against Rusty's door, stuck down with a piece of sellotape.

"I'll go and find her." Emma shot off, brushing away fresh tears.

Brook House mattered. The people. The horses. There was character here. Real love and concern.

"I respected you." I couldn't hold it in any longer. It didn't matter if I got banned now. There was nothing to get banned from.

Mrs Brentford swivelled round, achingly slowly, every trace of spirit drained from her face. I paused, momentarily taken aback, and then remembered the horses. "How could you? How could you sell out to a builder?"

The words hung in the air. An accusation. A betrayal. I needed an answer. An explanation. "I could understand it if there were no bookings, but

93

Guy's turned all that around, every lesson is full. The ponies are loving it, they've got a new lease of life, a sense of purpose."

I broke off, clenching my hands into tight fists, frustration making it difficult to speak. "H-how can you take that away from everyone? How could you let us build up our hopes?"

It was ages before she answered. For one moment I thought she was going to throw me out. Then her eyes softened and she flopped down into an armchair. "I'm sixty-nine years old. I've got arthritis and a bad hip. We might be busy at the moment, but come the winter it'll be the same old story. Horseworld has us beat, they've got the facilities. All I've got is a pile of debts and a tumbling down yard full of geriatric animals. I shouldn't even be telling you this. I don't have to answer to a twelve-year-old girl. I've been here for thirty years – don't you think it's a hard enough wrench?"

I swallowed hard, my turn to listen, knowing there was another side to the story but refusing to hear. "When I was all ready for quitting you told me I was feeling sorry for myself. You made me pull myself together when everybody else was just being nice. Well now it's my turn." I gulped, desperately unsure but deciding to take the bull by the horns. "Don't give up on Brook House, Mrs Brentford, not now, when it's really got a chance. We need you, the horses need you, and you wouldn't be happy living anywhere else. Because if you stop fighting, what else is there left?"

Sophie was waiting anxiously as I came out of the house. I shook my head but she already knew from my face that it hadn't done any good.

"They exchange contracts next week," I gulped. "I should think they'll want to pull down the stables straight away. They've been after Brook House for years."

Sophie stood tall, shaking like a leaf and clutching a skull cap covered with blue velvet. "Well, then I've got to take Minstrel to the Horse-world Show. It's our only chance." Her hands trembled as she slammed down the cap, pushing her hair behind her ears. "If I keep my part of the deal, Dad might just buy Brook House. There's still time – we've got a few days."

"It's a long shot." I held back, not wanting her to build up her hopes.

"Jodie, I've got to try. I've got to do everything I can to save Rocket and the others. Now, please will you teach me to ride my horse?"

Minstrel powered round the arena, flicking out his toes, ignoring Sophie's leg aids, but keeping one eye firmly fixed on me, standing in the centre. Sophie clung to the reins, her body rigid, telling Minstrel to go forward with her leg but confusing him by pulling on his mouth.

"You've got to let him flow," I shouted. "Drop the inside rein and push him forward with your inside leg."

Sophie collapsed through her shoulder and had to grab hold of the pommel to keep her balance. Her face was white and tight with fear but she kept on trying, determined to succeed.

"One, two, three, four. One, two, one, two." I counted out the rhythm to walk and trot, trying to get her to relax and loosen up. If you tense in the saddle the horse immediately picks it up and it sets him on edge. It was Sophie's nerves which made it so difficult for her to ride Minstrel. She didn't trust him like she trusted Rocket.

"Come on, Soph, don't give up." Emma led Buzby on to the arena. He was staring goggle-eyed at Minstrel, now trotting on the spot, which is called "piaffe" in dressage terms. Sophie completely lost her concentration and shot up his neck.

Rachel followed leading Rusty, dry-eyed but her face still red and puffy. Emma had found her crying her eyes out in the hayloft.

Now Minstrel had an audience he really started showing off, arching his neck and extending his trot, turning in his quarters and trying to pirouette round. Stallions are always more powerful and lively than geldings but Minstrel seemed to have rockets under his hooves. It made my heart thump just watching him.

Buzby was in total awe, obviously convinced that Minstrel had oodles of street cred.

"Come on, Minstrel," I murmured. "If only you knew how important this is."

Rachel circled Rusty and did a perfect rein-back. Suddenly I had an idea.

"Take Minstrel behind Rusty," I yelled, crossing my fingers behind my back. Rusty was an old schoolmaster and he might just be the steadying influence that Minstrel needed. Within seconds Minstrel dropped to walk and followed Rusty's lead, copying his every move.

"It's working!" Sophie was ecstatic. "I can ride him!"

And at exactly the same moment another idea formulated in my mind. Brook House might be closing down but the ponies deserved one last chance, they'd all worked so hard at their re-schooling.

"Let's take them all to Horseworld," I blurted out, excitement brimming up as my thoughts gathered speed. "Let's show everyone that it's not about breeding and bloodlines, it's personality that counts and good riding."

Emma's mouth dropped open and then snapped shut again.

"We can hire the ponies for the day and hack there," I babbled.

"But what about the roads?" said Rachel despondently. "You haven't been out since your accident."

"We can help each other," I enthused. "That's what the Five Pack is all about, isn't it? We can do it. I know we can. Let's show everybody. Let's go out on a high note."

"We'll be like a posse." Emma started to look dreamy.

I held out my hand and Rachel put hers on top. Then Sophie. Then Emma. Finally Rusty nuzzled his chin on Emma's hand as if he approved.

"That's settled then. We're going to the Horse-world Show!"

# Chapter Ten

"Dad might just keep Monty." A flicker of hope glimmered in Steph's eyes when we told her our plan. "I've never won a rosette before." Emma was determined that every Brook House pony was going to pick up a rosette, even if it was just for clear round jumping.

It was Guy's morning off so we'd agreed to help Sandra out by doing all the mucking out and hay nets. He was as upset as we were about the ponies being sold.

"It's growing back." Sophie came out of Minstrel's stable, convinced his mane had grown a third of a centimetre.

Emma was studying an article in *In the Saddle* on how to ride a showjumping course and still couldn't grasp how to turn direction in mid-air.

"I'd just concentrate on clearing the jumps." Steph laughed, ruffling her hair and making a face like Buzby.

We were all trying to think positive but it wasn't easy. Steph had driven us mad all morning taking photographs of the horses with her dad's camera but at least it had taken our minds off what was happening. And for the first time ever she didn't boast about it. I couldn't imagine Steph becoming a close friend but without Kate's influence she seemed to be turning into a nicer person.

"I hope Rachel's all right." Sophie glanced at her watch, her eyes narrowing. Rachel had become so quiet and withdrawn and she was spending every second with Rusty. "She should be back from the field by now."

"Hello, is anyone there?" A high-pitched, tinkly voice came from outside. Then we heard a car door bang. A customer.

Two women with a baby in a pushchair were glancing round the stable yard, uncertain. "We're looking for an instructor called Guy Marshall?" The one with the baby hesitated and then pulled something out of her handbag. "Someone put this on our windscreen and we'd really like to book some lessons – there are ten of us."

Emma nearly choked on her sandwich, then grinned at me as if to say I told you so. The photo-copied sheet on Guy and Brook House fluttered in the woman's hand, slightly torn where it had been caught by the windscreen wiper.

"Also," the other woman prompted, "we've all got children who'd love to join the Young Riders Club. Where do we get an application form and how much does it cost? We think it's a brilliant idea."

We all stared at her in amazement, and then Sophie started to explain that it was Guy's morning off but that Mrs Brentford should be somewhere in the house.

"You're wasting your time," Steph snapped suddenly, ignoring Sophie's dig in the ribs. "The riding school's closing down. All the horses are homeless and they're going to pull down the stables and build bungalows. It couldn't get any worse, we'll never be able to ride again." She turned away, her eyes filling with tears and her jaw trembling. I'd never seen Steph get emotional before.

"But that's terrible." Both women looked horrified.

"What was that?" Emma stiffened suddenly.

We could definitely hear shouting.

"It's coming from the back field," muttered Sophie, moving forward. I immediately imagined trespassers, hooligans frightening the horses.

"We saw two men in suits with measuring sticks if that's any help," announced one of the women. The voices were getting louder. Definitely men's voices. And someone else. Someone familiar. Rachel!

We charged across the yard. Buzby, Archie and Rocket were huddled by the gate, tails held high, staring across the field towards the trees. Suddenly, between two old oaks we saw Rachel riding Rusty bareback with just a head collar and lead rein. There were two men close by, stumbling away from her through a patch of nettles. Rachel urged Rusty on – she was riding straight at them!

"Rachel!" Sophie screamed.

My brain whirred with panic. She'd completely lost it. Sophie was the fastest runner and streaked ahead of the rest of us.

"Get out of here, go on, get out! Get out!" Rachel blazed, her voice husky and cracked with emotion. Rusty shied to one side, skewing his head upwards, and spinning round, confused and frightened.

"No wonder this place has gone belly up," said one of the men. "The quicker these nags and interfering kids disappear, the better."

"Leave her alone," shouted Emma, fiercely protective of Rachel.

"They were measuring out the field," Rachel spluttered, finally coming to a halt.

"They were frightening the horses and they shouldn't be here."

"I could report her for assault," threatened the man. "I could have you all done. I'm sure Mrs Brentford would want to know about this."

"Leave it, Greg," said his colleague. "We'll come back another day. They're just kids after all. Come on, we're due back at the office."

"Good riddance," Emma yelled, undaunted.

"We've got to stop them!" said Rachel, tears starting down her cheeks. But this was the hard, cold reality. The riding school was going to close down. It was inevitable. I saw Sophie's face crumple under the pressure. Our only chance was her dad.

"Did they give their names?" Steph asked abruptly, her eyes flashing with excitement. It seemed a really insensitive thing to say.

"Oh get real, Steph," Emma snapped. "It was hardly a polite conversation."

"I was just curious," she said pouting, but her mind was quite clearly buzzing a hundred miles away.

"You are a seriously weird girl," Emma threw back at her, but for once Steph didn't retaliate. She was too busy fiddling with the lens on her camera which was still slung round her neck.

"There is something we could do." She dropped her voice almost to a whisper.

"What?" Emma sneered, ready with a cutting reply.

"Nothing." Steph clammed up, her face going blank. "It was a stupid idea anyway."

Guy and Sandra helped us with all the preparations for the show and Mrs Brentford decided to spend a few days with her daughter, at least until the stables were sold.

In an effort to cheer us up, Guy told us endless

stories about life on the showjumping circuit and all the famous riders. Guy was just starting out with two novice horses which were Danish warmbloods, and he had to make as much money from teaching as he could.

He showed Rachel how to do deep-breathing exercises in case her chest tightened when she got nervous and gave me some warm-up exercises to keep my leg loose and relaxed. It was very similar to what my physio had suggested. With the regular daily exercise I'd only suffered with cramp once since my first day and that had been in the middle of the night.

"Where's Rachel?" Emma munched on some crisps while cleaning Buzby's bridle. The show was the day after tomorrow and we'd all started to get really nervous.

This was the first day of the holidays that Rachel hadn't turned up. And for that matter neither had Steph. It was ten o'clock on Friday morning and Guy was in the arena doing a group lesson. Sophie was parading around in a hacking jacket which she'd bought in a second hand shop for five pounds. She had an allowance from her dad which meant she could buy whatever she fancied, but she hardly ever used it. If Sophie wanted she could be really big-headed but she never was which was probably why she was so popular.

"This is weird." I came back out of the office after

answering the telephone three times in succession. All three people had been offering homes for the ponies and saying how horrified they were to read about it in the paper.

"What's going on?" asked Emma.

The phone rang again, and at the same time a car turned into the drive. Steph leapt out of the passenger door clutching a newspaper and waving at us like crazy through the window.

"I have a distinct feeling we're about to find out."

"That was someone wanting to take Rusty." Sophie came back from the office nonplussed. "She seemed to think he was about to be put down."

"Steph, what have you done?" My voice sounded cold and strained.

Oblivious to any problem, Steph, grinning like a Chesire cat, slapped the newspaper down on the saloon table and swivelled it round so we could all read the front page.

**RIDING HAVEN TO BE RIPPED UP FOR HOUSES. FIVE GIRLS FIGHT TO SAVE THEIR FOUR-LEGGED FRIENDS.**

Underneath was a picture of Rachel and Rusty chasing off the two men.

"Oh my goodness!" Emma slapped a hand across her mouth. "You took this picture."

"And I went to the newspaper." Steph proudly

105

pointed at the text. "They've quoted me almost word for word."

We all sat and stared. Sophie went to answer the phone which rang and rang.

"Don't you see?" Steph thrummed her finger against the article. "This is going to save the stables."

"It's Mrs Brentford." Sophie slid back into her seat looking white. "She's read the Weekly Gazette and she wants to speak to you."

Steph jolted slightly, her excitement slipping away.

"I'm not joking, Steph, there's fireworks coming down the phone. I think she mentioned something about skinning you alive."

"Jodie, there's someone to see you," Mum shouted up the stairs.

I was in the middle of dusting my model horse collection and after that I planned to try and make a hay net out of some baling twine I'd brought from the stables. I glanced through the net curtain but didn't recognize the red car outside. I knew all the cars belonging to the girls' parents, apart from Rachel's, as she always arrived alone.

"It's Rachel!" Mum shouted even louder. I could tell by the edge in her voice that something wasn't quite right. I came out to the edge of the stairs and Rachel was already halfway up, her eyes red and swollen.

"I'll take Mrs Whitehead into the sitting room while you have a little chat," Mum said in her "stepping on eggshells" voice.

My brother opened his bedroom door, took one look and shut it again, turning up Oasis on his annoying new CD player.

"Take no notice," I grunted. "He's going through the change – into an alien."

Rachel collapsed on the edge of the bed, turning her hands over and over in her lap. "I should have t-told you," she stammered. "You're going to hate me."

"I don't think so." I sat back, somewhat startled.

"I've lied to everybody and now I'll never be able to s-see Rusty again." Tears were flooding down her face, and she struggled to hold her voice steady. "Nobody knew I was going riding. I told Mum I was going to Grandad's. And Grandad I was staying at a friend's. Mum saw the newspaper and went mad."

"Oh." I sat silent for a few moments, lost for words.

"Mum won't let me go near the stables again. She wraps me up in cotton wool, she won't let me do anything. It's not fair. If she let me live my life for once I wouldn't have to sneak behind her back."

"And did Kate know all this?" I asked.

"How did you guess that?" Rachel glanced up.

"Just a hunch. I remember when I first met you, you looked terrified when I suggested we come to the stables together, and it was obvious Kate had got some hold over you."

"Yeah, she knew. Like a fool I told her. That was before I realized she was such a toad. Here." She pulled something out of a carrier bag she had brought with her. "I bought this for Rusty. I was going to give it to him just before the show." It was a bright red head collar with a matching lead rope.

"But you are still coming? I mean, you've got to talk your mum round."

"That's mission impossible." Rachel managed a half smile. "Mum's convinced horses are dangerous and they'll give me an asthma attack. She won't change her mind. I'd better go. It was all I could do to get her to bring me here."

"But you can't just leave." I started to panic.

"I'll stay in touch, I promise."

"Rachel!"

She was down the stairs and out of the door before I even had chance to get her phone number. I was left holding Rusty's head collar which must have cost an arm and a leg. Poor, poor Rachel. And poor Rusty. I couldn't quite take it in. Surely the last thing Rachel needed was to be cut off from horses. Even if she had deceived her mum?

*

"There's someone to see you." Guy came straight up to me as soon as I arrived at the stables the next morning. "She's round by the field gate. Oh and Jodie, go easy on her, eh?"

I truly expected to see Mrs Brentford, or possibly Rachel. I was amazed when I saw who it really was.

She had her arms wrapped around Archie's neck. He was gently nuzzling her shoulder in delight.

It was Kate.

I felt myself stiffen visibly.

"I know I'm the last person you want to see," she said, hesitating, "but I've got to speak to someone."

Archie moved away and Kate dropped her eyes, overcome with embarrassment. "It's about Horse-world Centre – I've been having some riding lessons there."

I flinched in surprise, although on second thoughts, it wasn't really much of a shock.

"Jodie," she began, fidgeting nervously and fighting for the right words. "You'll never believe what's happening there . . ."

# Chapter Eleven

"She's making it up," Emma said flatly. We were huddled in the saloon trying to absorb what Kate had told us. "It's so over the top it can't possibly be true."

Kate was waiting in the tack room until we'd reached a decision.

"After the pack of lies she's told us, how can we believe a word she says?" Steph said what we were all thinking.

"It adds up though," I said thoughtfully. A niggling hunch wouldn't leave me alone.

Kate had told us that at Horseworld they were buying young unbroken ponies cheap from the sales and banging them straight into the riding school where they quickly picked up what to do from the older ponies and were worked so hard that they were too tired to play up. They were then sold after a few months for huge sums of money as potential show ponies.

"That's why they were all so good-looking and well-bred," I burst out. "They didn't look like riding school ponies because they weren't. And that's why one was only three years old. I think it's true, for once in her life I think Kate's telling the truth."

Sophie pursed her lips. "But what about the rest? If that was really happening . . ."

Kate had told us that if they had particular trouble with a pony they resorted to doping it. Amazingly, there hadn't been an accident yet, but the show was coming up. Kate had overheard a conversation between the owner and the head instructor and hadn't dared go back since. But then she read about Brook House in the paper and knew she had to speak out.

"Anyone can fall into the trap of telling lies," I said, thinking of Rachel. "She deserves another chance."

Steph and Emma scowled.

"If we can expose them," I whispered, hardly daring to believe it, "the council will close them down. It's a lifeline for Brook House."

"We'll, tell Guy," Sophie said decisively. "He'll know what to do."

"We're not letting her back into the Five Pack until she's proved herself." Emma was adamant.

"Well, what are we waiting for?" I jumped up, feeling suddenly that everything was going to come right. "We haven't got a moment to lose!"

"I thought I knew what sheer terror was when I failed my maths assignment." Emma came out of

Buzby's stable looking pea-green. "But this is far worse."

I didn't tell anyone that I'd already been sick three times, and it wasn't the show that was scaring me to death but the ride there on the roads.

I was to take Rusty in Rachel's place because he was foolproof and the one I trusted the most. It didn't seem right without Rachel but we were all careful not to say so. I tacked up Rusty and fitted his new red head collar under his bridle so we could tie him up if necessary.

Guy was taking Minstrel in his horsebox because we didn't have a clue how he would behave on the roads. Sophie was riding Rocket who I was going to enter for the jumping when we got there.

I stared in front of the mirror in the outside cloakroom after redoing my white show tie for the sixth time. "You can do it, you can do it, you know you can, you can," I chanted away to the mirror like I used to when I was younger.

"How did it happen?" Kate appeared behind me, leaning against the doorframe, interested but not mocking.

"I became friends with a girl who thought horses were for showing off with. We were out riding one day and she dared me to ride down the middle white line on a quiet road. Anyway, I did, a car came, and my pony reared and then fell on my leg. The car swerved. Nobody else was hurt, but from the knee down my leg was a mess."

"I'm sorry." She really did seem to mean it.

"Listen," she said awkwardly, "if you help me get Archie round the clear round jumping, I'll help you get down the road. Deal?"

"A problem shared is a problem halved." I managed a smile, suddenly feeling quite tearful. I stuck out my hand and she gave it a stilted shake.

"Jodie, before, when I was a pig . . ." She paused. "Well, the truth was I was jealous. You seemed to have everything – you could ride really well, you were popular and you didn't seem scared of anything."

"Well, I was." I grinned, feeling my cheeks tighten. "I still am."

"I know." Kate smiled warmly and it made her look so much nicer. "I was horrible to everyone because I hated myself. I made up those stories because I didn't want to be ordinary. But you know, now that I am, it's quite nice. Because you don't have to pretend. And it's a lot easier to keep friends."

"Yeah, I know." I thought of Rachel, isolated.

"And I can honestly say, if there's a gate or a treble in the clear round I shall curl up and die."

"You can do it, you can do it," I repeated under my breath. Rusty steadily put one hoof in front of the other as cars whizzed past. Most drivers were fantastic and slowed right down but the odd one hardly seemed to notice us at all. Kate was on my outside riding Archie who had to keep waiting for Rusty who was smaller and had a shorter stride. Sophie was ahead on Rocket, and Steph and Emma behind on Monty and Buzby.

I was doing it. I was facing up to my fear and overcoming it. Just. Beads of sweat trickled down the inside of my white shirt and my hands shook as I clasped the reins.

Sophie waved her right arm up and down to slow a lorry and I wanted to close my eyes as it crunched past. Rusty didn't bat an eyelid.

"Just another mile or so." Kate registered my lifeless face. "You're doing really well."

I decided at that moment to take the BHS Road Safety Test and learn how to be totally responsible on the roads.

Cars and trailers streamed into the showground. There were far more people here than we ever imagined.

"He's there!" Emma yelled her head off as she spotted Ash Burgess, the celebrity guest chatting to Guy by the horsebox. "What a babe!"

I practically had to stuff a riding glove in her mouth to stop her wolf whistling. Buzby who was wearing a bright red browband with matching numnah and bandages decided to set off after a pretty bay mare who had just deposited her rider by the secretary's tent. Archie was more interested in someone dressed up as a chicken carrying a huge chocolate egg than in romance.

"That's my fancy dress costume!" Emma was hoarse with outrage. "What am I going to do now there's another chicken? I'll be eliminated!"

"Oh, I don't know." Sophie smothered a smile. "It could be the start of a beautiful friendship."

Guy had all the extra equipment we needed so we made our way over to the horsebox where Minstrel was kicking pieces out of the sides. Ash Burgess disappeared which was hardly surprising with six eager girls riding towards him.

We had told Guy everything about Horseworld Centre and he had listened and formulated a plan. We trusted him completely and he hadn't once doubted us. Everything was in place. In the meantime, our job was to show everyone how brilliant the Brook House ponies really were.

"Look at them," exclaimed Emma. A posse of riding school riders came from the stables, all the ponies wearing matching numnahs embossed with the Horseworld logo. "How on earth are we going to beat them?"

The clear round jumping had already started in ring one and the lead rein class had just finished. "It will be me next," gulped Steph as the tannoy announced the best ridden 13.2hh and under. Guy had entered us all for our various classes.

"I can't do it," Sophie moaned, wilting against Rocket's shoulder. "I can't ride Minstrel, I can't. I must have been crazy to even think it."

Right on cue Minstrel half-reared, lashing out with one of his hind legs against the horsebox side. Sophie squirmed with fear. Emma shuffled awkwardly and toyed with Buzby's reins. Two girls strolling past giggled behind their hands. We just caught a few snatched words . . . "Wouldn't be seen dead on any of them . . . The grey one looks like my grandad's wolfhound."

Emma went bright red in the face and took a step forward.

"Take no notice." I grasped her arm.

Kate and Steph's confidence shattered like broken glass.

"Come on, girls, don't let them get to you." It was so obvious they were crumbling. "We're better than any of them."

"Oh yeah." Emma rolled her eyes. "Says who?"

I was losing them.

"We'll be a laughing stock," Steph mumbled.

Rusty yawned, resting a hind leg, looking tired out before he even started.

"Don't give up now," I pleaded, "not now we've come this far."

Emma's eyes hooked onto something by the

entrance gates. A wave of excitement ran right through her.

"What is it?" We all followed her gaze.

"It's Rachel!" Steph finally croaked in disbelief. "And she's wearing her jodhpurs!"

Rachel was hurtling across the grass field, arms flailing and a huge grin plastered across her face.

Rusty perked up, jerking his head towards her voice.

"I can ride!" she yelled out, catching her hairnet which was slipping down her neck. Rusty started whinnying and wouldn't rest until he'd licked her face, devoured six polos and happily sucked her hair, his chin resting on top of her head.

Emma gave Rachel a hug and then we all did, apart from Kate who shuffled awkwardly with embarrassment. "I don't know what your mum said to mine," Rachel ran on, chattering non-stop, "but it did the trick. As long as I have my inhaler I can ride whenever I want." She gave Rusty a kiss on the nose for good measure and pulled down the stirrups.

"Shouldn't you be getting ready?" She glanced at Rocket and Buzby and Archie grazing with their saddles propped by the horsebox. "It might be my imagination but I thought we were going to wipe the board?"

"She's a different girl," said Sophie hopping

nervously from foot to foot, clutching her arms to her chest, even though it was a warm day.

Rachel was in a corner of the field with her mum, warming up for the best ridden. Rusty was putting every ounce of concentration into helping her as much as possible. Guy was giving Kate a few words of encouragement, especially after Archie tried to roll in a cowpat and she lost her stirrups.

"Come on, Mrs Brentford, where are you?" I scanned the showground for her birdlike figure. She had to come, she just had to!

"Oh no." Sophie went as white as her show shirt and her eyes filled with panic. "It's my dad!"

"A clear round for Brook House Buzby!" the tannoy bawled out as Buzby hauled Emma out of the arena before she could even collect her rosette. Steph shot forward and grabbed the orange ribbon before a pretty Welsh Mountain pony devoured it in one gulp.

"We did it!" Emma dangled round Buzby's neck, patting him non-stop, her riding hat slipping off in the process. "Our first rosette!"

Buzby had hurled himself round the clear round course giving everything a wide berth and nearly unseating Emma at the spread. It was only a fluke that he had taken the right fence at the end because Emma's hat had tipped over her eyes and she couldn't see a thing.

"It's Mum and Dad!" Emma suddenly pointed to two people striding towards us waving a thermos flask and a camera. Emma slid off Buzby and overcome with emotion promptly burst into tears.

"I'm not riding Minstrel." Sophie threw back her head and openly defied her dad. He was a big man with an intense gaze, huge bushy eyebrows and a shock of black hair. Just looking at him intimidated me.

Sophie stuck out her chin, her cheeks flushed. "All you think about is winning, being the best, but it's taking part that counts. Rocket might be common and ordinary to you but I love him and I'm going to ride him – and I don't care if we come last because I'm going to enjoy every minute of it. He's ordinary-looking and with no great breeding but has a heart of gold and that's the most important thing. And I know you don't love me and you think I'm useless but it's my life and I've got to do my own thing. All I ever wanted was for you to be proud of me but more than anything else I want to be proud of myself." Sophie broke off, gasping, her eyes shining.

I ducked down to put some hoof oil on Rocket, feeling as awkward as a fish out of water but neither of them seemed to notice.

"Oh you daft little sugar," Her dad's voice cracked as he opened his arms and Sophie flew into them. "You're the kindest, sweetest person I've ever known. How could you possibly think I don't love you?"

# Chapter Twelve

"You're riding Minstrel!" Steph charged up from the secretary's tent, her fair hair hanging over one eye. "Sophie had your name down all along – she's taking Rocket in the novice."

A rush of adrenalin scorched through my veins and I had to stop myself screaming out loud. I was riding Minstrel. I was riding Minstrel! It was a miracle!

"Come quick!" Emma tore up on Buzby who now had the orange rosette pinned to his bridle and was walking three hands taller. "It's Rachel, she's been pulled in first in the best ridden."

"Keep calm, Rachel." Steph clasped her hands together as the first four ponies showed off their skills in reverse order. After the initial parade around the judge the competitors had to do a display in walk, trot and canter, usually with a figure-of-eight and rein-back and sometimes an extended trot. Archie wasn't even in the running in the back row.

"Kate's going to be livid," cried Steph, her eyes dancing at the thought of trouble. "I'll bet a bumper

121

burger with triple onions that she'll go mad when she comes out."

"Done." I shook hands, hoping that Kate really had changed.

Rachel moved off on Rusty, keeping her shoulders back and her hands really still.

"She's concentrating like crazy." Emma latched on to my arm.

The secret was to blank out the fact that you were at a show with people watching, and pretend you were schooling in the field back at home. Rachel visibly relaxed as if she'd just remembered. Rusty strode out and did the best show of his life. It didn't matter that he was old with grey hairs and a stringy body. He was trying every second, straining to help Rachel, and flexing his neck like a dressage horse.

"He's beautiful," Emma croaked, who always welled up at anything emotional. Even Buzby behaved and stared at his stable mate as if to pick up tips.

Rachel was awarded the first rosette which was such an achievement for someone who had just started riding. Kate got nothing and Archie sidled out of the ring in disgrace.

"Here goes." Steph winked, but Kate proved everybody wrong and went straight across to Rachel who was still gawping at the rosette in a daze.

"Well done." She held out her hand. "You did brilliantly and you deserved to win."

Rachel looked stunned but soon started grinning. "I was hoping, well, maybe we could start again as friends?"

"It's that pony!" I seized Emma's wrist, my eyes trailing a familiar pony with a white blaze. It was a chestnut, the one I'd seen at Horseworld staggering about.

Now it was plodding along in first gear behind two other ponies with a novice rider on its back who didn't seem to know anything. It didn't take much working out. Rachel and Steph read our thoughts instantly. Kate wheeled Archie round, her face set in a grim line. "That's the one," she said angrily, "that's the pony that's being doped."

"Where's Guy?" Emma nibbled on her thumbnail, scouring the showground for the slightest glimpse. Any plan we'd had was disintegrating before our eyes. He should have been here by now.

"We can't do anything yet." Kate's voice was loaded with warning. "You heard what Guy said."

The novice jumping was well under way with a fat cob exploding out of the ring after sixteen faults. I had to focus on Minstrel. This was my big chance to prove to myself once and for all. I couldn't blow it.

"I've got to go!" I swallowed hard with nerves.

Kate read my thoughts immediately and volunteered to help. "Are you sure this is what you want?" She touched my arm with real concern.

A group of people had crowded round the horsebox where Minstrel was snorting and stamping, looking about to burst out of his skin. His neck was arched and he was straining on the lead rope. He'd never looked more beautiful.

"I'm perfectly positive," I told her, striding purposefully up the ramp. After all, how many people got to ride a pure-bred Arabian stallion?

"He's nuts." Two girls jolted back against the ropes as I rode into the collecting ring with Minstrel swinging his quarters first one way and then the other, and then moving sideways in the perfect half pass.

"Whoa boy, steady now." I was shaking with nerves.

"Jodie!" Sophie yelled, and rode Rocket towards us. "It's all sorted out," she gasped, "Dad's finally listened, he's even talking about buying Rocket. Isn't that fantastic?"

She didn't mention anything about the riding school.

"That's brilliant," I said and really meant it.

Suddenly a gasp went up from the ringside viewers and Minstrel leapt in the air as if he'd been touched with electricity.

"It's Steph," cried Sophie, standing up in her stirrups. "She's fallen off."

I had no idea she was even in the ring.

Emma ran up, dragging Buzby. "Steph's bombed out," she shouted.

Steph rode out of the ring, grass-stained and close to tears, with Monty looking bewildered and slightly shaken. "I know I've let everyone down," she gulped, obviously overhearing Emma's remark. "Why don't you all have a good laugh, eh? Stupid old Steph who falls at the second fence. Well go on, I know I'm useless." Her face crumpled and she kicked Monty forward towards the horsebox, desperate to get away.

"Leave her." I stopped Emma following. "Just give her a few minutes, she'll be OK."

"Poor Steph," said Rachel as she appeared on Rusty, "she was trying so hard."

"It's you!" Kate rushed up, checking Sophie's show number. "They're calling you, you're in next!"

"Oh crikey." Sophie dropped her whip and went white. "Where's Dad?"

"Whoa boy, steady boy." Minstrel froze, I could feel each muscle grow taut like drawn elastic.

"She's over the planks," Emma commentated, balancing on a cavaletti jump to see, while Buzby tore at some juicy grass.

I forced a smile onto my rigid face and tightened

125

the reins. Minstrel was about to explode. And then I saw why. The chestnut we'd spotted earlier was sidling up to Rusty with a vicious expression on its bland face, one hind leg poised ready to lash out. Minstrel erupted in rage. I clung on as best I could as he flew forward with his teeth bared, and cannoned straight into the chestnut's quarters.

"What the hell?" A man wearing a Horseworld sweatshirt dived forward. The girl on the chestnut burst into tears. Rachel stared stunned as Rusty escaped injury by the skin of his teeth. And it was all thanks to Minstrel.

"You fantastic, gorgeous horse," I cried, flinging myself forward, patting Minstrel's thick, crested neck and praising him until I went hoarse.

"It's dangerous, that horse," someone yelled out. "It's a stallion!" Then there was pandemonium.

"There's nothing in the rules to say that a stallion can't enter," Kate yelled back at the man in the sweatshirt.

"I run the show, sweetheart, so I should know."

I got off Minstrel and tried to calm him but all the shouting was driving him wild. Rachel brought Rusty alongside, which seemed to quieten him a little.

"Where's Guy?" Emma was on the verge of tears. A woman with an unstable hairdo was threatening to throw out all the Brook House riders.

"That's because we're beating them hands

down." Steph pushed forward with Monty, her eyes red-rimmed but set with determination. "You can't throw us out," she cried, and glanced round, almost manic, "because there's something you all ought to know—"

"Guy's coming," Sophie interrupted as she pushed Rocket through the crowds, her eyes blazing with triumph. We'd completely forgotten about her showjumping round. "That's the pony," she yelled, pointing wildly at the chestnut.

A look of horror darkened the face of the man in the Horseworld sweatshirt.

"Hallelujah!" Emma punched the air with her fist as Guy and Mrs Brentford appeared behind Rocket. Mrs Brentford pulled herself up to her full height, a smirk playing on her lips. "Graham Harris, we have reason to believe that you have been illegally doping riding school horses."

"You interfering old bag, how dare you?" He sprang forward. "I'll sue you for slander."

"I wouldn't try it." Sophie's dad stepped up, twice the size and doubly fierce. "You see, we have a vet here and a council official. It seems you have a record for breaching your licence more times than most people have had hot dinners."

"We're saved!" Emma leapt round Rachel's neck, clinging on like a monkey. We all fell together in a scrum, clutching each others' hands, our cries of delight mingling with Emma's screechy laughter. I had a dreamy grin on my face and Sophie was happier than I'd ever seen her.

"The Brook House Six Pack for ever!" Emma yelled, scaring Buzby who was tied up to the horsebox, trying to peel the varnish off with his teeth.

"Does this mean I'm reinstated?" Kate asked, trying to disguise her anxiety.

"Of course." Sophie smiled warmly. "There's no need for secrets, or pretence any more – we all know each other, warts and all. From now on, we'll be there for each other – like real friends."

Kate put an arm round Rachel's shoulder. Then we all put our hands together and swore agreement.

Brook House Riding School was saved. So were Rocket, Buzby, Archie, dear old Rusty, Ebony Jane, Frank and all the other gorgeous horses I'd grown to love. They wouldn't have to be split up, not ever.

Mrs Brentford wasn't selling out to the building company. Neither was she retiring. Sophie's dad had agreed to fund the school as a silent partner. Horseworld Centre would lose its licence for sure and three people had already come up to us and asked about the Young Riders Club. We referred them to Kate as reigning president.

Archie had attracted quite a fan club already and desperately tried to look shamefaced when he stole a little girl's ice cream. All the ponies were thoroughly enjoying the show and even Buzby was being well-behaved, with an over-docile expression on his face, which no doubt meant he was plotting his next trick.

Guy had raced back to the school to fetch Frank so that Mrs Brentford could enter the veteran in hand class. The show was carrying on because there were too many people there demanding that it should.

The only hiccup was that Minstrel had been relegated to the open class because a complaint had been lodged that he was over 14.2 hands. After being measured by the vet it turned out that he was fifteen hands with shoes. There was no rule to say that a stallion couldn't enter but the course for the taller ponies was far too big for us to manage.

I was sick with disappointment but elated for Sophie who with no pressure from her dad sailed round the novice to get fourth place and a green rosette and grooming bag.

Kate plucked up courage to enter the pairs clear round jumping with Emma and we pushed her into the ring with Archie who gawked at the tiny double as if it were a fire-breathing dragon. Kate set off tight-lipped and wooden with terror, but by the final fence she was jumping her socks off and loving every minute. Archie played to the spectators as only he could.

"You were brilliant." Emma shook her hand as

they rode out and then threw herself round Buzby's neck.

"Did I really say I was too scared to jump?" Kate grinned wildly, pushing back her riding hat and buzzing with the thrill. "From now on, Archie, we're going to have a jumping lesson every week, even if it means cancelling *Teen Dreams*, cleaning Dad's car and mowing the lawn."

"Jodie!" Guy strode up, catching admiring glances from all surrounding females but barely noticing. It made me feel important and temporarily deadened the sting of disappointment.

"Mrs Brentford says if you don't ride Minstrel in the open, she's going to ban you from Brook House and Sophie's dad is backing her up."

"You're joking." I almost gagged. "You are joking, aren't you?"

"You can do it!" Sophie squeezed my arm, followed by Emma and Rachel in a state of hyper-excitement.

"I'll talk you through the course," promised Guy, narrowing his eyes, gauging my reaction. "It's not that big, honestly. Minstrel can do it with his eyes closed and so can you."

Fear knocked me sideways and then suddenly gave way to a new feeling of recklessness. What if I didn't try? How would I feel riding home knowing that I hadn't given it a go? Minstrel deserved a chance – we both did.

"I'll meet you at the main ring in two minutes." Guy shot off, striding up to the secretary's tent.

"Remember how you first rode Minstrel when nobody else dared?" Kate looked at me with such intensity.

"Yeah, and remember how I dropped Frank's saddle when my leg seized up?"

"That won't happen." Kate practically grabbed hold of my shoulders and shook me. "It's mind over matter."

Steph was already brandishing my riding hat and gloves.

"You lot are nothing but a pack of overbearing bullies, do you know that?"

"Yep." Emma and Sophie frogmarched me forward. "It's all part of the Six Pack service."

"Two more to go and then you're in." Guy re-designed the practice jump to make a spread.

I'd never felt more sick in my life. My insides were churning up until I had to bend over the pommel of the saddle and clutch my stomach. Guy pretended not to notice. If I was sick now I'd never live it down.

"They're falling like flies," Emma reported back, filling me with confidence – not! Sophie altered my stirrups and Kate read out quotations from her diary which was supposed to make me feel better but didn't.

131

By now a wave of anxiety was crashing around inside me. I desperately wanted Mum to turn up but there was no sign. She'd promised to be here an hour ago.

A seventeen-hand, lanky thoroughbred with a giraffe neck, loped out of the ring with four faults. Amazingly there hadn't been a clear round yet. Guy said the standard of riding was appalling and the course was so flimsy, a fly could knock a pole down. I didn't care. At least when I blitzed every jump it wouldn't be quite so embarassing.

Minstrel floated round the practice ring, delighted to be finally taking part and quivering with excitement. Even worse, every person in a hundred yards radius was staring at us.

"The greatest form of defence is attack." Mrs Brentford appeared from nowhere, beaming from ear to ear and reminding me of a little leprechaun or maybe a fairy, only she'd look ridiculous in a tutu. "Forget about your leg and it will forget about you," she whispered.

"Two minutes and then you're on." Guy cast an anxious glance at Minstrel. My teeth were chattering. "Hold him off the road jump and get a straight approach."

"Guy," I whispered, suddenly cracking altogether, "I don't think I can do it." I was convinced my left leg would be useless and Minstrel would take off in the ring. I just couldn't go through with it.

I was struggling to dismount when Mum's voice pierced across from the other side of the ring. I blinked in surprise when I saw who was there beside her. It was Dad. They were both waving frantically. I tried to wave back but was suspended half on, half off, as Minstrel danced on the spot and I desperately tried to scrabble back into the seat.

But everything was OK now. A lovely exhilarating warmth was flooding through me. Mum and Dad were here. They were still smiling as the loudspeaker crackled and spluttered and then called in number 37. That was my number.

"Ladies and gentlemen, we have with us a very special young lady who has overcome a terrible riding accident and debilitating injuries. This is her first time back in the ring and I'd like you to put your hands together and give a very warm welcome to Jodie and her young horse Minstrel."

I nearly died. Clapping broke out all round the ring, someone cheered and whistled and I saw Guy clapping with his hands above his head and Mum sticking up her thumbs. She wasn't freaking out, even though I was on horseback.

So this was facing up to my problem? Somebody had done this deliberately and I could bet all my post office savings it was Mrs Brentford. But somehow it wasn't too bad. I wasn't dying with embarrassment. It was no longer a huge secret. I didn't feel resentful or angry. I'd come to terms with my accident and moved on: I wasn't feeling sorry for myself any more, I was living my life.

"In you go, love, be quick." The steward guided us into the ring.

Minstrel seemed to sense my new peace of mind and walked quietly towards the start. I heard a group of girls gasp and admire Minstrel's beauty. But then I was sitting on every girl's dream – a chestnut Arabian stallion, and only I could ride him.

The first fence loomed up. Then the second. My leg didn't seize up. Minstrel listened to every aid I gave him and apart from missing out a stride at the double he did a perfect round. Nothing came down because he gave everything a foot to spare. Minstrel proved that he wasn't crazy or uncontrollable but a first-class showjumper who just needed some understanding. We both proved something in those few minutes which would stay with us for ever.

"You were brilliant!" The whole of the Six Pack went crazy as soon as I rode out of the ring. People were still clapping as I dismounted. All I could think of was Mum and Dad. And then suddenly they were there, wrapping their arms round me and kissing my hair. We clung to each other for what seemed like ages and I really couldn't speak. Minstrel was furious at being ignored and clonked me on the head with his chin.

I won a small silver trophy, a rosette and a red

cooler sheet for Minstrel which clashed with his chestnut coat.

Mrs Brentford came and congratulated me and then dashed off to the veteran class which she won with Frank who knocked spots off everybody at the grand old age of 22. Nobody was quite sure whether the veteran award was for Frank or Mrs Brentford!

Emma came last in the fancy dress mainly because Buzby had eaten all her tail feathers and she had fallen off trying to flap her arms like a chicken. Steph did incredibly well in the gymkhana races, picking up a fourth, a third and a second in the flag race. Altogether we'd collected thirteen rosettes, two trophies and countless horsy items between us. Not bad for a bunch of ponies everybody had written off.

I surprised even myself by linking arms with Dad and strolling round in Sophie's Union Jack shorts without feeling the slightest bit self-conscious. It turned out to be Kate who had tipped off the commentator. She eventually admitted it after chasing Archie round the beer tent for half an hour.

"Jodie!" Sophie charged up just as I had finally found a few moments to thank Minstrel for the best day of my life. "Something incredible's happened," she gasped. "Are you listening? This is so important."

"You have my undivided attention." I tried to keep a straight face and failed.

"Dad wants you to have Minstrel on loan. He'll pay all the expenses. You can have him as your very own horse – we won't have to sell him." She gave me a hug and then Minstrel, and searched my face for a reaction.

I could feel the emotion building up like a tidal wave about to sweep through my body, but for the moment I was numb.

"Jodie?" Sophie's jaw went slack and she narrowed her eyes in panic. "Don't you want him?"

And then it came. Dizzy, heady euphoria that had me dancing round the horsebox, clutching Sophie's hands, tears of happiness and relief springing up in my eyes.

"It's j-just the best," I stuttered, my mouth collapsing so that I sounded unintelligible. I mumbled another sentence and Sophie's face clouded over in confusion. Minstrel half-heartedly kicked his partition for attention.

I blew my nose and took a deep breath but all that came out was a whimper. "I said . . ." I paused, struggling to find composure.

Sophie's nose twitched as she tried not to laugh.

"I was going to say . . ." I paused again, and then deliberately raising my voice to mega-decibels, I shouted, "Brook House is the best riding school in the world!"